INFLAME ME

RAVAGE
motorcycle club #4

Wall Street Journal & USA Today Bestselling Author

RYAN MICHELE

Fourth Edition Published: October 13, 2019
ISBN-13: 978-1-951708-03-0
ISBN-10: 1-951708-03-2
ASIN: B0145S7I0W
Previous Edition Information:
First Edition Published: 2015
Second Edition Published: 2015
Third Edition Published: November 17, 2017
ISBN-10: 151735319X
ISBN-13: 978-1517353193
ASIN: B0145S7I0W

CONTENTS

Age is but a number...

With no other choice, **Tanner** must seek out the one person she's never met, but gave her **half of his DNA.** In going to him, her world **opens wide** to a life she'd never experienced, the **Ravage MC.**

Whether she realizes it or not, she just **gained an extended family.**

Danger lurks in a **tall, tatted, older, scary as hell man** that could crush her with one hand. Except, looks can be deceiving. **Wolf in sheep's clothing they say.**

Rhys knows what he wants the instant his eyes land on Tanner and **will stop at nothing to have her.**

Even if that means going up against his best friend and brother, her father. **Nothing** and **no one holds him back.** Except maybe himself.

When push comes to shove, Rhys always shoves back **harder, faster,** and **fiercely.**

Survival of the fittest doesn't apply to Rhys. He **will survive** with his woman at his side, or **die trying.**

Come and join the ride with the Ravage MC!

To all of you who love the Ravage Family just as much as I do.

NOTE FROM THE AUTHOR

I know I teased you like crazy at the end of *Consume Me* with my evilness. I would say I'm sorry, but I'm truly not. It was never my intent to write Rhys's story, but when he started talking and Tanner started screaming, I had to put the words to paper.

I want to thank each and every one of you for taking the time to read my books. I appreciate you more than you will ever know. Thank you.

Enjoy and find out who Cameron Wagner is ...

1

TANNER

"TANNER?" MY MOTHER'S WHISPERED VOICE COMES ACROSS the phone.

My body tenses immediately, going on alert, and the smile adorning my face dies instantly.

"Mom, what's wrong?" I ask, pulling over to the side of the road. I wasn't going to pick up the phone since I was driving, but when my mom's name popped up on the screen, I had to answer. In life, there are certain people you don't put off answering a call from, and my mother is number one for me.

"Baby, I need you to come and get me." Her voice is so muffled it's as if she's covering the phone, afraid someone will hear.

"What's going on?" I fear the answer she is going to give me. In the pit of my stomach, I can already hear the words that will escape her lips, and I don't want to hear them. I never want to hear them.

"James has been drinking again."

Fuck me.

The asshole said he was going to AA, claiming he was getting his addiction under control for my mother. Unfortunately, James is a violent drunk, not one who passes out or can function on the stuff. He is downright nasty.

The first time I saw marks on my mother and questioned it, she did what she always does: covers for him, makes excuses for him, blames herself for why she's so badly bruised she can't go out of the house for a week.

I told her that, if it ever happened again, I would take her the hell out of there and wouldn't give a shit if she wanted to come or not. If I had to duct tape her to the car to get her wherever in the hell I took her, I would.

"You have got to be kidding me," I snap a little too harshly into the phone. I can visualize my mother flinching at the tone. I dig deep and take a breath, needing to calm myself for her sake. There is no sense in adding to my mother's pain, especially when she called me for help. "I'm on my way. Is he there?"

James is a big man, and when I say big, I mean five-eleven and between two hundred fifty pounds to three hundred. The thing with him, though, is he can move and do it fast. He's been trained for years by the police academy, after all.

"Yes," she muffles into the phone, a slight tremor in her words. "He's passed out in the living room."

Crap. Their living room is where their front door is, and from the way their house is set up, even the back door can be seen from there. Getting my mother out might be tricky without waking him, but I'll give it everything I have.

I throw the car into gear and begin the twenty minute drive to her, keeping her on the phone with me.

"Gather up what you need, Mom. Throw it in a garbage bag if you have to. Be quiet and move quickly." I pause, pain splitting my heart in two. "Can you move ... quickly?" What if she's hurt to the point that she can't move? Oh, God.

"I ... I'll try." She groans roughly over the line and sniffs her nose, no doubt crying. I would love to reach through the phone and take away her pain. On to plan B.

"Where are you in the house?" I maneuver the car in and out of traffic, feeling like every precious second away from her is a second too damn long.

"Bathroom. I locked the door." A small bit of comfort comes from that, even if the flimsy lock wouldn't keep James away from her if he really wanted in.

"Stay there. Don't come out. When I get there, I'll pack for you, and then we are gone." Where the hell are we going to go? I have no clue yet. I do hair for a living, so it's not like I have elaborate exit plans for escaping from a cop who's supposed to love my mother. That's a lie right there.

I knew the first time he put a hand on her that he didn't, but she was too damn infatuated with him to listen. I'll do what I always do—figure it out as we go, moment by moment. That's what I do: I fix it.

"Okay." Her voice comes out weaker than only seconds before, and I fear she may pass out on me. If he hit her in the head, she could have a concussion. I have to keep her alert, with me.

"Mom, keep your eyes open. Do you hear me?" She mumbles something. "How bad is it?" My heart squeezes. I can't lose my mom. I just can't. She's the only thing I have in this world.

"I don't think he broke anything, but it's not good, Tanner. Really not good."

Rage bubbles up, but I push it down. Now is not the time for it. I have to get my mother out of there, then, and only then, will I let that flow through me.

"Okay. I'll be there soon. Stay with me."

The light ahead is red, and I'm getting pissed off at the stupid thing for not changing. Why won't it change? There are no other cars coming down the road. Change! All right, so I'm losing it a bit. I can't! *Be strong, Tanner.*

I shake my head and begin to tell my mother about the woman who came into the shop today, wanting a huge change with her hair, going from blonde to brunette with pink and red highlights. My mother's breathing is steady, and every once in a while, she'll say something in the phone, acknowledging that's she's listening. I question her often, keeping her as alert and awake as possible.

Finally, I pull up to the one-story, tan house with green shutters and beautiful landscaping around the front with flowers in bloom everywhere. Isn't it amazing something that looks so pretty from the outside is hiding something so dark on the inside? But isn't that how it always is? Judging a book by the cover. As long as it looks good, there's nothing wrong. It's just like people.

Everyone looks at James as an upstanding man, serving and protecting the town of Anglewood, Tennessee. No one would ever suspect he did this to my mother. No one. They would more than likely ostracize my mother for even claiming such a thing.

"Mom, I'm here. I'm coming up," I tell her, hanging up the phone and throwing it into the passenger seat. I briefly thought to call the police for help, but as quickly as it entered my head, it left. With James's all-American boy status around here, I know they won't do shit and will simply turn it around on my mother. Then she would be stuck. I won't allow that. She's out.

I kill the lights before fully getting up the driveway, not wanting to make noise if I don't have to. Lights illuminate the home with only a few of the drapes closed, the living room being one of them. I turn off the engine and get out of the car, only shutting the door enough to turn the dome light off on the inside. I have never really had to do this quiet stealth thing before. Hopefully, I can pull it off.

Peering through the window of the living room, I see James lying on the couch, half on it and half off. His wide mouth is open, and drool is falling out and onto his blue T-shirt that has a huge wet puddle. Gross. I never thought for a moment that he was good-looking, but my mother saw something in him. What, I didn't have a clue. Still don't.

I open the screen door with a slight creak and cringe at the sound, wanting to yell at it to shut the hell up yet simply staring at it angrily. Turing the door handle, I find that it's locked. Shit.

I pull my keys out, holding all the keychains and keys hanging from it to silence them, and then open the door slowly. My eyes stay locked on the man on the couch as I creep through the living room, into the kitchen, and back to my mother's bedroom.

My heart constricts as I look at the room. The lamp on the side table is turned on, but it's crashed on the floor, the shade hanging on to it by a thread. Clothes, blankets, jewelry, papers—well, everything is tossed to the floor, and the mattress is partially exposed. But the kicker is the blood on the sheets. Quite a bit of blood is smeared on the fabric, and it's bright red. Shit.

I move to the bathroom door, but I don't dare to knock.

"Mom," I whisper softly, holding the door handle, my other hand on the top of the door, and my ear pressed to the door, trying to listen. "Mom, it's me. Open up."

I hear slow movements on the other side of the door along with some muffled groans. Then I feel the lock click in my hand, and I turn the handle.

Oh. My. God.

My entire world stops and tilts on its axis. This isn't a beating. This is so much more than that. Her beautiful face is almost unrecognizable with bruises forming and cuts with blood oozing out of them, falling down her face, into her eyes, and down her cheek. Her long, strawberry blonde hair is matted to her face with the blood. Her clothes, for lack of a better word, are ripped and torn in so many placed it looks like she's wearing tattered rags.

"Mom." I bend down in front of her, not wanting to touch her yet wanting to desperately, just to make sure she's here with me.

I jolt my hand back, clutching it. I can't add to her pain, and nowhere I touch her would help right now.

Tears form in my mother's eyes, but she doesn't shed them. "Baby, get me some clothes, and I'll get dressed while you pack things."

I seriously don't think she could dress herself judging from the way she's holding her arm and the pain etched in her face. She said she didn't think anything was broken, but I'm seriously rethinking that one.

Instead of arguing, because God knows how much time we have until James wakes up downstairs, I nod, unable to form words. I then get her some baggy clothes, hoping like hell they won't hurt too badly.

Everything from that second on is a flurry of activity on my part. I grab two bags from the shelf in her closet and begin hastily throwing in my mother's things, grabbing shirts, pants, shoes, and everything in-between.

Opening the dressers, I continue with the packing. Well, it's not really packing, more like swiping the entire drawer and stuffing, but whatever. I toss my mother clothes in hopes that she will be able to get them on her, but if she hasn't by the time I'm done, I'll help her.

It takes me less than five minutes to pack up everything of my mother's that I can see and enter the bathroom. She's sitting on the toilet seat with a towel blotting away the blood on her face.

"Mom, once I get you out of here, I'll get you cleaned up." I kneel down before her and slip on her tennis shoes, tying them quickly as her body trembles. I have to get her out of here before whatever control she has erupts. "I have two bags packed. Is there anything else you need?"

Her eyes lift to mine, tears pooling in the green depths of them. *Please don't cry.* If she does, I'm afraid whatever strength I have will dissipate, and I will follow.

What child wants to see their mother hurt? Not me. Tears would do me in.

"There's a box. I hid it in the corner of the closet. You need to peel back the carpet from the right corner and pull up the plank that is beneath it. Inside is a shoe box. I need you to get it and my purse, but that is in the kitchen, so we can get it on the way out." Even though her voice is strangled with pain, I can sense the strength within my mother in her words. God, I love her.

"Stay here," I order, moving quickly back to the closet and doing exactly what my mother said. I yank the yellow box out, which has a bit of weight to it, but I don't have time to look. Instead, I grab another bag, one that has my mother's gym clothes in it and throw the box inside.

I pile all the bags by the doorway, and then it hits me. Can she walk out of here, or am I going to have to carry her? There's no way I can carry the bags and her. Hell, I can probably barely carry her. Double Shit.

Mom listened, staying right where I left her in the bathroom. Her eyes meet mine, sorrow blooming in them. Enough of this.

My adrenaline pumps through my veins, and as it courses, all I can think of is getting her out of here now.

"Can you walk?" I move to the side of her body where her arm doesn't look like it's hanging on and help her rise to her feet as she inhales quick pants. Talk about a tough woman. I'm not sure I would be able to be this strong after what she has endured. It's another thing I've always admired about my mother.

"Yeah," she says weakly, taking a step before her knees buckle a bit.

I hold her weight as she regains some of her balance and is able to walk a few more feet. After a bit, she's doing much better about getting her legs moving.

I grab the bags, hoisting them over my shoulder and picking up one in my hand. Mom stays by me as we walk slowly through the house.

Entering the kitchen, I spot my mother's purse on the

counter. "I'm going to get it, so I want you to lean against the chair for a minute."

My mother nods at my whisper.

I glance at the couch to find he's gone.

James is gone.

Panic spreads through my veins like wildfire as I search around frantically. I grab my mother's purse and fling it around my neck. "Back," I whisper as I meet my mother halfway from the chair she was holding.

"You fucking bitch!" James's angry growl comes from behind me as he yanks my ponytail and tosses me across the room like I weigh nothing.

As I crash to the tile, the wind momentarily gets knocked out of me. I look up to see him slap my mother across her face before she plummets to the ground in a boneless heap.

"Get up!" he screams at her, kicking her hard in the ribs.

Asshole.

I get up—my whole intimidating five-foot-four self— drop my mom's bags, and stalk toward them. He senses me coming and turns around, moving lightning fast and striking me across the face. I fly through the air as pain sears my lip and cheek. The metallic taste of blood seeps into my mouth, and I lick it. Luckily, I didn't hit anything on the way down from his horrible punch.

James begins to really punch and kick my mother as tears stream down her face.

"Leave her alone!" I scream, getting his attention.

"What? She's a fucking bitch. You, on the other hand, would be nice to have." As a devilish gleam shines brightly in his eye, I get the feeling he's not talking about using me as a punching bag.

He lands one more blow to my mother then begins to stalk my way. I look around the kitchen for something, anything to use to make him go away. I have no doubt that, if he gets me down to the floor, it's going to be over for me, for my mother. There's no way I can fight off his bulk, but I refuse to give up.

Continuing to scan the room, I move backward as he continues to come toward me.

"Don't run. This will be fun. I promise you'll enjoy it." His smarmy ass actually licks his lips, and bile comes up my throat, burning the back of it. No way in hell.

I eye the knives in their tidy, little, wooden block holder on the counter and make my way toward them, keeping one eye on James.

"Stay away," I tell him, but it falls on deaf ears. If anything, the words make him happier, like I'm a challenge; and that's the last thing I want him to think.

I grab the biggest knife out of the holder, placing it in my left hand and a smaller knife in my right.

"Aw, you think you're gonna hurt me with those?" He flat out laughs, but it's so sinister it sends chills up my spine. "I can disarm you with those in a second," he gloats. I know he's right. He's trained for this. I, however, am not. Hell, I've never held a knife to another human being ever. I'm not sure what in the world I'm doing.

The adrenaline pumps through my veins as I try to steady my shaky hands. If I want me and mother to live through this, I'm going to have to do something, but what?

My hands tremble as I clutch the knives, knowing

they are my only lifeline. "Go away, James. Just leave. Get out of here." I'm wasting my breath, though part of me hopes he will just leave and go away to some other place, disappear like some miracle from above. Tough luck there.

"Fuck no. I'm just getting started." His steps get closer, his fingers turning into fists.

Without thinking, I throw the smaller knife at him, the blade entering the left side of his chest by his shoulder. He stops, momentarily frozen, as if my throwing the knife at him wasn't even on his radar.

"You just threw a knife at me, you little cunt," he growls, not removing the knife. His furious eyes pierce me, almost knocking me back a step. Oh, God ... There's nothing like pissing off a raging bull.

I move the other knife to my right hand, needing more control of it. The adrenaline inside, along with my mother's safety, fuels me.

With his bulky arms at his side, he comes closer, the menace in his face reminding me of The Hulk. I try not to let the fear show, but I'm pretty sure I'm doing a shitty-ass job of it.

"Stay away," I say again with a tremble in my voice. Dammit, go away!

"You fucking little bitch. You're just like your mother. After I'm done fucking the shit out of you, I'm going to kill you right in front of her then beat the fuck out of her some more."

Burning. I feel like I'm burning. The fear is still there, but fury masks it, pulling me into a red-filled haze. He will not hurt my mother again.

I point the knife in front of me, directed toward him

as I run to the other side of the room. I just have to get my mom up and out of here. It's possible, right? No. No, it's not possible. Shit!

He charges at me, this time at full speed. The knife in his shoulder is not slowing him down a bit, and I'm not quick enough. He grabs my arm holding the knife and presses some part of my arm that is so damn painful I have no choice except to drop the knife and hear it clatter to the tile floor.

No. No. No.

He pulls my side up against his body, and I smell the alcohol on his breath, my stomach churning from its potency. He keeps ahold of my arm while punching me twice in the stomach, knocking the wind out of me. If he weren't holding my arm, I would have collapsed to the floor in a heap.

"You're as stupid as she is. Let me show you how I make sure your mother knows her place in this house."

I begin to fight and struggle out of his grasp, using my arms to hit, nails to scratch, and legs to kick. Even drunk, he's got great reflexes and deflects all of them, putting in a couple more slaps and a kick of his own to my shin that bursts with pain.

"Stop!" my mom's hoarse voice says from the floor as she tries to pick herself up from it, but she doesn't make it far and collapses again.

"Fuck you, Mearna. Your daughter needs to be taught that she shouldn't put her nose in other people's business, let alone put a fucking knife in me." His next punch is a doozy, knocking me hard to the tile floor as he fully lets go of me. This one was to the chest, right between my breasts, and I feel like I can't breathe. At all.

I gasp, trying to suck in air as he leaves me on the floor, heading toward my mother.

"Guess I need to shut you up first before I fuck your daughter," He barks at her.

With all the strength I can muster, I scan the floor, looking for the knife. It couldn't have gone far. With James's back to me, I hold in all the grunts of pain, being as quiet as I can. I find it on the other side of the kitchen island. Gripping it with all my might, I rise to my shaky feet, still remaining quiet, letting the anger give me strength.

"Bitch!" he yells, sending a shattering blow to my mother.

On instinct alone and as quickly as my messed up body will take me, I make my way over to his back. My brain shuts down, and all I hear is my mother's cries. Holding the knife with both hands, I raise it high and begin to plunge it into his back. He screams in pain, and I get two more jabs in and out of his flesh before he turns around.

I step back as he lunges toward me. Then I stick the knife out, and it pierces his chest.

"You bitch." This time, he gurgles the words.

I pull up on the knife that is inside his body with a strength I didn't know I had in me as he falls to his knees. I keep pulling as blood coats my hands. I must have hit his heart or some major blood supply because the white tile around us instantly becomes red.

James makes one last attempt to grab my feet, but I pull the knife out of his body and jump to the side, my body screaming at me the entire time.

He falls to the floor in a loud thud while my heart

pounds, and my blood stained hands shake. What did I just do?

"Tanner!" my mom says from the floor, lying there in the fetal position, snapping me out of my new discovery.

I watch James to see if his chest rises and falls, and when it doesn't, I slowly make my way over to him.

"I've gotta make sure this is done," I tell her in a blank voice that I've never used before. It's as if I'm a different person, allowing her to take over my body for the moment. It's like the me I've known my whole life decided to leave my body.

"Let's just go. Let's get out of here," she says in haste. "I don't want him hurting you, Tanner," she pleads, bringing me slightly back from the fog, but not much.

"Mom, if he's still alive, he's going to come after us. If he's dead ..." I trail off, knowing then the cops would be after us, and it would be one giant cluster-fuck that I don't know how to fix. First things first—keep us safe.

I walk over to James, the knife still clenched in my hand, and make my way to his face. His cold, brown eyes stare back at me, unmoving. I don't want to touch him, but I have no choice. I put my hand under his nose to check his breathing, and nothing happens. I place two fingers on his wrist and check for a pulse, or I try to since I've never had to do this before and have only seen doctors and nurses do it. I move my fingers around a couple of times, but I don't feel anything.

He's dead. And I killed him.

2

TANNER

As I wipe the blood off of my mother, the tub turns pink. I wanted to do this in the shower, but I knew I wouldn't be able to hold her up on my own for that long. My entire body aches from James's blows, and I feel like I'm a robot doing what needs to be done then moving to the next step, whatever in the hell that is.

I wash her hair then help her out, wrapping a towel tightly around her frail body. Every part of her has some type of welt or bruise that will only get worse in the next couple of days.

I brought her back to my small apartment, wanting to get cleaned up. She protested, saying we needed to go to a hotel and do it there, but I didn't listen. I was in too much of a fog after taking James's life. I still am.

Mom goes into my bedroom where I help her put clothes on, careful not to hurt her even more. I need to take her to the emergency room, but I just killed a cop, a well-respected one at that. If I take her, I'll be arrested for his murder, and I can't risk that.

As my mother lies down, I try to figure out what in the hell I'm going to do. The rational part of me says that what I did was self-defense, but no one will believe me.

My flight instinct is pumping hard, wanting to escape from the mess that my life just turned into. I get into the shower and wash all of James's blood off, the swirling of pink going down the drain into nothingness. My body aches, but I can't focus on that. I have a few bruises, but nothing I can't cover with clothes. However, my face will take a lot of makeup to cover the bruises beginning to form, and I'm not sure how I'll fix the split lip.

It won't take long for the police to find James once he doesn't show up for work, and when they do, it will be hell.

I shake my head, letting the water flow down me as if to absolve me of my sins. I took another human's life. Sure, he was a worthless piece of shit, and I'm not sorry he's dead; I just can't believe I had it in me to do it. If you would have asked me if I did, I would have said hell no, but I proved tonight that, when push comes to shove, I can.

Before leaving my mother's house, she ordered me to get the knives and even the wood block where she stored them to bring them with us. Why? I didn't ask. I just did as she said. I turned all the lights off in the house then put my mother and her things in my car. I didn't turn on the headlights until I was pretty far down the road and didn't see anyone around.

My hands trembled the entire way home, and my mother was eerily quiet. Even in the tub, she was. I'm sure she's thinking right along with me. What do we do now?

I turn off the shower and pull myself together, throwing some sweats on and an old hoodie. I put the towel on top of my head, wrapping it around my hair before I enter the bedroom where Mom is lying down with a miserable expression on her face. Can she be sad that I killed him? No, surely not. The look on her face is concerning, though.

"Mom?" I question, nearing the bed and sitting down next to her. "Do you want me to take you to the ER?"

Her head rises, and she gives me a slight smile. "No, baby girl. We can't do that. You and I both know this was self-defense, but the guys at the station are not going to think that way." Her confirming my thoughts makes a rock form in the pit of my stomach, weighing me down. "He's head of the good-ol'-boys club, and they aren't going to let this slide even with this kind of defense."

I feel sick. I can't go to jail ... to prison.

"What are we going to do?" I whisper, not having a clue where to even start. I don't have any friends who could get us out of this or help us. I only have a couple from work, but they wouldn't know the first thing about what to do next.

I lean back on the bed and stare at the popcorn ceiling, the softness doing nothing for the nerves racking my body.

"We are going to see your father."

My head snaps to hers, and I instantly feel woozy. *Don't move so fast, Tanner.* I blink my eyes, trying to clear the dizziness. My mother never talks about my father, never told me who he is, never says a word about him, ever. In my twenty-three years of existence, I've asked about him maybe four times, and each time, I was met

with, "You don't need to worry about that." Our relationship is close, almost like sisters instead of mother and
daughter, so I knew she was doing it for a reason, but I
never questioned her. For her to say we are going to see
him is more than a shocker. I'm surprised my heart didn't
stop for a few seconds. Then again, maybe it did, and I
didn't register it.

"What?" I ask, my words coming out a bit snippier
than intended.

She sighs. "I'm afraid he may be the only one who can
help us out here, but we need to go quickly before James's
shift comes up in two days, and they notice him missing."

Confusion sets in. How can my father fix this mess?

"How would he know what to do and who is he,
Mom?"

"I'll explain on the way. Pack some bags with whatever you will need for a while and anything that you
absolutely won't want left behind." She can't be serious.
We are going to go on the run?

"You're scaring the shit out of me. Are you saying that
we won't be coming back?"

"Baby, I don't know what is going to happen. Right
now, even with my battered head, I'm trying to come up
with ways to protect both of us. Your father is the only
option I see right now. We need to get on the road. Now."
Her eyes widen in the mom way that tells me she's dead
serious.

"Okay, but you will explain all of this, Mom," I
concede without backing down. She will tell me.

"I will. You also need to put the clothes we were both
wearing and the knives in plastic bags and bring them
with us." How the hell would she know to do that?

"Mom, you are really creeping me out here," I tell her, getting up and throwing clothes in a bag. Am I on some episode of CSI or something?

"Tanner, I'm not even getting started."

WITH THE GPS set to Sumner, Georgia, we've been driving for the past five hours, and I'm getting seriously tired. My eyes keep drooping, and I have to pinch myself to stay awake. My mother fell asleep almost as soon as she got in the car. I gave her some of my left-over Vicodin from when I got my wisdom teeth pulled before we left, and it wiped her out. Since I wanted her to rest, I haven't bothered her, but with the little machine telling me that we will be there in about an hour, I need answers. I need to know what I'm getting myself into.

"Mom." I gently tug on her hair, not really knowing where I can touch her that won't cause her too much pain. She stirs in the seat, her groggy eyes opening slowly.

"What?" her voice comes out hoarse and crackly.

"We'll be in Sumner in about an hour, and I need to know what's going on before we get there." I keep my eyes on the road ahead of me. The sun rose a while ago, and my sunglasses shield the brightness. I desperately need coffee and a bathroom almost as badly.

"I never wanted you to know him," she says on an exhale. "He's not a very standup man."

"And James was?" I say in a clipped tone, a bit too harshly, but come on here.

"Point taken, but your father is different."

When she pauses for too long, I look at her. "Keep going. We've only got an hour."

"Your father is Cameron Wagner. He's part of a motor-cycle club called Ravage. Let me start from the beginning." I nod. "I met him when I was very young. He was much older than me, and I fell hard for him. He was just joining the club at the time, and I didn't know much about it. I thought it was like a riding club because he was always riding his Harley everywhere. I loved being on the back of that thing." She pauses for a second, seeming to be caught in her memories.

"For about a year, we lived together while he was joining, and I stood by him every step of the way. Long story short, I found out that he was into some really bad things. I called him on it; he told me it was none of my business; and we split up. He joined the club; I took off. Once I got settled, I found out I was pregnant. I never told him."

There is so much more I want to know, so much more to this story than she's saying.

"You say you lived together for a year, and the only reason you split was because of this club?" I ask, piecing the puzzle together.

"That man had my heart and soul," she whispers so softly I don't think she wants me to hear her, but I do.

My heart clenches for her. "You loved him."

Her head turns to me, and a soft smile comes to her lips. "Yes. I loved him very much. It killed me to leave him. If it weren't for you, I probably wouldn't be around anymore."

My breath seizes in my lungs. Did she really just say what I think she said?

"Mom, you're saying you were going to kill yourself?"

The words get lodged in my throat and come out very croaky, but I somehow manage to get them out just as fear almost pulls me under.

She stares out at the open road, lost in thought briefly. "At the time, I was young and naïve about the world. I saw good and bad, nothing in between. When I learned one night that what he was doing was on the bad side of the coin, I thought I had to leave. I didn't want to, but in my gut, I had to."

"What did you see?" I'm a bit sacred of the answer, yet I'm too curious not to ask.

"That doesn't matter." She shakes her head, wiping the thought away. "I did. He never followed me, so I knew he never felt the same way about me as I did him." My heart breaks for my mother. "Once I found out I was pregnant, I picked myself up off the floor and got myself together."

"And you never contacted him about me?" I can't help feeling a little hurt that I know nothing of the man who is my father. I have never had to want for anything, but it still would have been nice to at least know him.

"No. He lives a different lifestyle than you or me. You'll see. It's not like what you know now."

"You act like he's in some kind of cult or something, Mom." I mean, seriously.

"Tanner, in your father's world, women have their place, and men have theirs. Some women can hack it, but I didn't stick around long enough to try ..." Her words dangle off.

"But you wish you had," I finish her sentence, watching as a tear rolls down her cheek.

"I wonder what my life would have been like had I

stayed. Would I be happy now instead of"—she looks down at her broken, battered body—"this?"

"Oh, Mom, I'm so sorry." Even if I am upset with her about not telling me about my father, I can't help having my heart break right alongside her.

"There's nothing for you to be sorry for. I made my decisions, and I live with them," she states firmly.

I pause for a moment, kind of confused about something. "Mom, we talk a lot." I look to her briefly, and she looks down at her hands. Then I move my eyes back to the road. "We've talked about the first time I had sex, our times of the month, when I had my heart broken—hell, even what I had for dinner the night before. In all those talks, in all those deep conversations, you couldn't tell me about my father, even if you didn't want me to meet him?"

I counted on my mother for everything. She's my confidant on every aspect of my life. I don't get how, after all this time, she wouldn't tell me about him. Then this happens, and he's the first person she thinks to run to? Why?

"I wish I could better explain it, Tanner, but I can't. I'm so sorry."

I hear my mom sniffle. I reach over and grab her hand as she sucks in a breath, forgetting for just a moment how badly she's hurt. I quickly remove my hand.

"It's fine, Mom. Let's just get you better."

Twenty minutes later, the sun shines brightly on the sign for Sumner.

"All right, Tanner, let's check into one of the small hotels up the road here. You'll give them a different name —whatever you want—and pay cash. Got it?" Something tells me she learned more from my father than she's willing to let on because I've never seen this side of her.

"I don't have a lot of cash on me, Mom." That was a stupid move right there. I should have gone to the ATM and pulled everything I could out. I did buy gas with cash, so that's a plus in my favor. I make a horrible fugitive.

"When you stop, get the box," she says.

I instantly remember the box from her closet, and I can't help wondering what is inside.

"Were you planning on leaving him?" I ask, thinking maybe it's money.

"I didn't know what I was going to do. I just needed it for a rainy day ..." She trails off. "And today, it's pouring."

I do as she says and get us into a small, musty-smelling room with a carpet that is straight-out-of-the-seventies orange. Mom told me to leave most of the stuff in the car, but bring some clothes. I helped Mom the best I could, and with each step she took, she gritted her teeth.

She's always been strong, working job after job to take care of me and still being there when I got out of school. There is no one better than her. No one. Faults and all.

"I want you to put on sexy jeans and a tight top."

I stare at her, my jaw slacked. Did she really just say that?

Her eyes meet mine. "Go with it," she announces like it's the final say, which it is since she's my mom, but really? I'm going to wear sexy jeans to meet my father? The thought of it is beyond strange. "You need to cover up all the bruises and marks that you can. Your split lip will be hard, but we can put fire red lipstick on, and it will cover it from afar."

"Why do I need to do all this? You know him; why don't you do it?"

"Look at me, Tanner," she says, her voice weak. "You're going to the clubhouse where I'm pretty sure he is. To get in there, you need to look sexy and hot. Once you get his attention, bring him out to talk to me. I'll take care of the rest." Her lip quivers, telling me she's nervous, which only makes me nervous.

"You sure this is a good idea, Mom?" I question as the pit of my stomach aches. Not only am I meeting my father for the first time, but I have no idea what I'm walking into.

"It's the best option we have right now. Cameron will know what to do."

WE PULL up to this massive warehouse thing with tall gates and barbed wire around the top. Maybe thinking this was a cult was right on target. The whole thing gives me an eerie feeling. The large, metal gate is open as cars line one side of the drive and bikes the other. To the left is a garage, and on the right, it looks like a big party area with people scattered all around.

"Mom?" My voice quivers with fear. My father is here, at a party?

People are scattered all around: women in barely-there clothes, couples making out and groping each other. It's like nothing I've ever seen, and that's just from the car. What the hell am I going to see when I get in there?

I throw the car in park and look to my mother for guidance.

"I can see in your face you're petrified. Get it out of your head. Confidence and head up. You are so damn strong, Tanner. I know what's happened has rattled you, but don't let it. Your father will help us. I know he will. I need you to walk in there like you own the place and plaster a smile on your beautiful face. The first guy you see with a leather vest on, you ask for Cameron Wagner. Got it?"

Do I have it? A huge part of me wants to scream to the heavens and run faster than the speed of light out of here, far from this. I can't, though. I have nowhere else to run to.

I pull out my inner bitch-with-'tude and nod to my mother. "Then what?"

"When you tell him who you are, he's not going to believe you. You're going to have to bring him out here to me." I catch that little tremor in her voice from the thought of seeing him. Holy hell, after all this time, he still affects her this much.

"Let's get this over with."

Mom reaches over and grabs my hand, squeezing it, her eyes flinching in pain, but I feed off the comfort of her touch. "Tanner, there is nothing to be nervous about. Since there's a party going on, I'd normally wait, but we don't have time for that right now." She's right, not that I know what the hell Cameron will do.

I suck in not only my confidence, but that of my mother. "I'm ready."

Walking up to the large door of a huge warehouse, my

mind whirls when I see several couples in various stages of undress. One woman is actually pulling a guy's penis out of his pants and bending down. Holy shit! I'm no virgin, but in public, at a party, with everyone watching? He has one of those leather vests on, but there is no way I'm asking him. Screw that.

I open the heavy, wooden door and am blasted with loud music, cigarette smoke, and the stench of beer. I blink my eyes, getting focused from the onslaught of light from the room. With my smile plastered firmly in place, I look around, getting the lay of the land before I move toward the bar. People are scattered everywhere. Some are on the dance floor, dancing provocatively.

"Hey, beautiful. Where you been all my life?" is said.

I turn to the voice. The man attached to it has blond hair pulled back tightly with a red, white, and blue bandana gracing the top and across his forehead. His long beard matches his hair and comes down to his chest. His mustache pretty much covers his lips, but I can still see he's smirking at me. Wrinkled lines surround his leathered face.

"That work with all the ladies?" I ask with a soft smile, not allowing a bit of the uncomfortableness to come through. I'm strong. I have a mission. I'm on it. Done.

"Only when I want it to." His hand comes out to my hip, and it takes everything in my power not to flinch from the touch because of the bruises he cannot see. He's not bad-looking, just a stranger. Since when do I allow strangers to touch me? Apparently, this is a first.

I look to his leather vest and decide it's time. "Maybe you can help me," I say as sweet as pie. It's better to have this guy on my good side and not the bad.

"I'll help you with whatever you need." The man takes a step closer, and I immediately feel a presence to the side of me. My eyes dart in that direction.

Holy mother of God. I can't decide if this is the scariest man I've ever laid eyes on or the sexiest. Hell, maybe both. His face is so intense, like grab you and never let you go intense. His blue eyes sparkle, but not in a pleasant way. No, like a predator of the night way, but they suck me in, nonetheless. His face is lined with thick stubble all around his strong jaw, his features aged with intent, and those lips ... I feel my knees begin to tremble as some sort of electricity floats in the air between us.

My already on-edge nerves seem to implode in my gut, spreading through my body like a wild fire. I clench my fists and reopen them as they dampen. My breath comes up a little short, and it takes me a moment to realize that I actually need oxygen. Never once in my existence has a man had this effect on me, and that is totally what he is—a full-blooded, older man.

I unlock my eyes from him, using every bit of strength I have to turn away, shaking my head and refocusing on bandana man.

"Thanks, but I'm looking for Cameron Wagner." The grip on my hip tightens painfully, and I wince because it's the hip I fell on earlier, or yesterday. Hell, I can't even remember. All I know is that it hurts.

Bandana man's eyes turn from lustful to scary fierce in the blink of an eye, and my confidence gets shaken a bit. "What do you need him for?"

Strong vibes come from my side again. I know it's

from the sexy, scary man, but I don't turn away from the one in front of me as my pulse picks up, and fear creeps in. I try to push it back, but it's growing. Hard core.

"I'm Tanner, his daughter."

Bandana man quirks his eyebrow, his hand relaxing a bit on my hip. The relief is immediate, but he still holds tight.

"No Cameron Wagner here," the man says.

Shock fills me, my mouth gaping as everything inside me begins to crumble. He has to be here. There isn't another option, no other choice, nowhere else to go.

"He's not here?" I tremble out, looking around the room in haste. My take-no-prisoners attitude slowly drops down, and if I had it in me, I would kick my own ass.

My mom was wrong. He's not here. He's not part of this club. We came all this way for nothing. What in the world are we going to do now?

"Sorry I wasted your time." I step out of bandana man's grasp and take one more look at the sexy, scary man whose eyes are narrowed on me. Great, nothing like making an ass of myself.

Escape. I need to get out of here.

I move to head for the door when a hand grabs me around my arm, and I flinch, the pain radiating throughout my body. I try not to show it, but come up short. I wasn't prepared for it, so it caught me off guard.

"What's wrong with you?" the deep baritone voice from the sexy, scary man asks, the sound of it penetrating all the way down to my bones, doing strange things to my body.

I let out a breath, the pain racing. "Nothing. I'm fine."

I'm not telling anyone what the fuck is going on here if I don't have to, especially to men who look like they could rip my head off at any given moment.

"You're lying," he accuses.

My strength is about tapped out for the day. The fight is about gone. I breathe in deeply and look into his eyes. Something inside them compels me to tell him. I don't know what it is, but it's there.

"I have a situation. My mother told me that I needed to come here and find my father Cameron Wagner so he could help us. Since he's not here, I'm not going to waste your time," I practically plead with the man, hoping he will let me go.

"Office," the bandana man's voice comes from behind me, making me jump and whip around. Oh, no. I'm not going anywhere.

I try to pull out of sexy, scary man's hold, but it's too tight, and with each movement I make, his grip tightens, only causing me more pain.

"We need to talk," he says, and my knees seriously begin to quiver.

"No, really. I didn't mean to bother you. I'll leave and never come back." Horrible, horrendous fear charges through me. If I go into a room with them, what will they do to me? I don't want that answer, really don't want it.

Sexy, scary man's lips come to my ear, and I quiver as his breath tickles me. "Relax. We just wanna talk. It's noisy out here with lots of ears."

I notice he said nothing about not hurting me or anything of the sort as he pulls me. I walk with him, his hand still attached to me. *Stupid, Tanner!*

With bandana man in front of us, I notice his long

braid comes down his back. The back of his leather vest says Ravage MC with a large skull in the center with flames coming out of the top. The word Georgia is on the bottom. The leather of the vest looks old, worn, and I bet pretty soft to the touch.

I can feel eyes everywhere, watching us as we move through the crowded space, both men and women's. This is not how this was supposed to work out.

My mother! I want to be pissed as hell at her, but I can't. She didn't know this wouldn't work, and all she wanted was to help us.

"In," bandana man says.

I move into a wood-paneled office holding a large desk with a computer on top. Pictures line the walls, but I only glimpse at them, focusing my attention on the man in front of me. The click of the door echoes in my ears just as all the music blasting through the place quiets down to a more tolerable level. The thump of my heart takes its place in my ears, though.

My arm is released, but the door is blocked by a wide chest, crossed with arms, each lined with tattoos. I look away and search the room for windows, a phone, even though I have no one to call, something. There is nothing. The windows are covered in bars, and if there is a phone, I don't see it. Dammit!

I shrink back from the thick, heavy tension in the room. I want to be the standup woman I know is inside me; however, something about these intimidating men makes me want to fall into myself. So not normal.

Bandana man strokes his beard thoughtfully. "You said your mother told you to come here?" I nod my head, words unable to escape my lips. "What is your mother's name?"

I absolutely do not want to give these men my mother's name. Shit, I already told them my first name, another stupid mistake. I don't speak, only stare.

"Look, Tanner, you need to tell us what the fuck is going on here. We don't like open-ended shit and definitely don't like it showing up at our doorstep. You tell us what's going on, and we go from there." It sounds reasonable when he puts it like that. In fact, his matter-of-fact tone is welcoming, comforting, even through all this chaos. Not that these men will help me, but if I at least tell them, maybe they'll let me go. Maybe.

"My mother's name is Mearna."

Bandana man takes a step back like I've slapped him across the face then punched the wind out of him. He sits on the corner of the desk, his hands coming to grip it tightly. His knuckles are so white I'm surprised he doesn't crack the wood.

"And how old are you?" he asks.

"Twenty-three," I say quietly, keeping my eyes on both the men. Even when I was stabbing James, I never felt this kind of fear for myself. For my mother, yes, but myself? No, not until now.

"Fucking hell!" Bandana man bellows, and I jump again at his furious words. "Mearna O'Ryan is your mother?"

I take another step back from him at my mother's full name. Holy shit, he knows her.

My lips move, but nothing comes out. It must be shock.

The presence that I've come to recognize as the sexy,

scary man comes to my back. His hands grip my shoulders, and I tense. Then he moves them up and down my arms, and as weird as it sounds, it is actually comforting. It takes a beat, but it really helps with the nerves.

"Yes," I whisper, answering him finally.

"You have got to be fucking shitting me!" bandana man booms, turning around to the desk and crashing everything to the floor in a huge sweep.

I step back, falling into a rock hard body with nowhere to go. My eyes widen as bandana man picks up a chair and throws it across the room like it's nothing. Then it smashes to the ground in a loud crash. The arms at my shoulders come around me as he leads me a few steps back toward the far wall.

Bandana man stands there, his chest rising and falling with obvious exertion.

"You about done? You're scaring the shit out of her." The man behind me says, and he's not lying. If anything, it brings back memories of James, only adding to my fear of this man.

"Fuck!" bandana man screams and turns around, his back to me. It rises and falls, his intakes of breath very audible in the room.

Shit, what have I gotten myself into?

"It'll be okay," is whispered in my ear, not helping much.

Bandana man turns around and stares at me, really stares, taking every single one of my features in, which I feel very uneasy about. This goes on for long moments while I stand here, feeling like I'm drowning, and all the while, my mother is outside in the car. God, I hope she's all right.

"You look just like her," bandana man finally says, and I gasp. "Same reddish hair, same rich green eyes. I should have known just by looking at you." He pauses. "She really think Cameron Wagner is your father?"

I suck in deep. "She's never told me his name until we were on our way here. I never knew about him. She said he's the only one who can help us right now. That's why we came here."

"We? She's here?" the bandana man questions, and my stomach falls. Me and my freaking mouth. How come I can't keep a lid on it? Oh, no, I seem to keep sticking my foot so far in it I'm surprised I'm not choking. No use in lying; they'll just go out to the lot and see.

"She's out in the car."

"Fucking hell!" bandana man says, pushing off the desk and going to the door.

I try to move, but the grip is still around me.

I have to stop the angry man.

"Wait, please. She's hurt really badly. Please don't hurt her anymore. Take it out on me, not her," I say in a rush, the words coming out like verbal vomit. I'll take the hits for her. I'll take whatever this big man has if it will protect my mother.

He halts, turning to me. "What do you mean she's hurt?"

I bow my head and shake it. I don't want to say it, but … "Her fiancé beat the shit out of her."

"Son-of-a-motherfucking-bitch!" he explodes. "You"—he points to me—"come with me. Rhys"—he points to the man behind me—"talk to Pops. Get this shit closed out."

The strong arms leave me, and coldness invades my

body. I immediately miss the comfort and turn to him, but he's already heading to the door.

"I'll tell Pops and be right out." As he leaves me alone with bandana man, I don't know why, but I want him back. I want him to protect me from this man who is so angry I'm not sure even my wonderful mother will be able to bring him down a few notches.

"Come on," he says, leaving the room.

I stand there for a moment, shaking my head, and then hurriedly follow him—well, to the best of my abilities.

He pushes his way through the crowd, yelling names as he goes. However, the music is so loud I can't make them all out. I think Cruz or GT or something.

We step out into the night and shoot to the parking lot. I have to take twice as many steps as him to keep up with his long stride.

"What car?" he barks.

"The blue one on the end." I try to get a step in front of him, but he's quick—I'll hand him that.

He knocks on the passenger side door, and I immediately jump in front of him, blocking him from my mother. I already stepped up to James for her; scared or not, I'll do the same for bandana man.

"Stop!" I scream, bumping him with my hip.

"Girl, you'd better watch how you talk to me," he says as my mother's wide eyes stare at me through the window.

"Stop it. She's been through enough. If you want to talk to her, fine, but she's hurt badly, and I can't take her to the ER, so just give me a minute," I lash out at him as the fear recedes, and my protective instincts kick in. No one hurts my mother.

I open the door.

"Cameron," my mother breathes.

I turn to bandana dude. He's my father? What the hell? He couldn't have just told me that?

3
___

TANNER

I glare at him then turn back to my mom. "He wants to talk to you, okay?" I tell her.

"Yeah," she whispers softly, her eyes still wide in shock.

I step to the side of the door as Cameron steps closer, the fury bouncing off him. Then he takes a look at my mother. "What the fuck happened?" His words are so cold, menacing, and scary that goose bumps form on my arms.

"Cameron," my mother says in a calm tone, surprising me. She must have come out of her shock.

"Do not call me that. It's Dagger. Second, tell me what the fuck happened to you? Tanner here said it was your old man?"

I close my eyes at the words, remembering only a few hours ago.

"Dagger? Really?"

"Not now, Mear. Tell me."

Mear? I've never heard anyone call her that. Ever.

She sighs, but there is confidence in it. Damn, I love her strength. "Bottom line is James got drunk. He used me as a punching bag, and Tanner came to help me. We thought James was passed out, but he wasn't. There was another fight, and he ended up dead."

Cameron—I mean, Dagger's—back straightens, and his face goes on alert. "Can you walk?" he asks her in a tone that is surprisingly caring. This night seems to be full of them—surprises.

"I need to help her," I say from the side.

"Fuck that." He picks my mother up as she closes her eyes tightly; no doubt, he's touching something that hurts her. He carries her bridal style as I slam the door to the car and lock it.

I trail behind them, and the guy Dagger called Rhys —what kind of name is that?—meets us as he's coming out.

"Call Doc. We need him ASAP. Find Princess," Dagger barks to another man as we enter. He has longish, brown hair and a beautiful brunette is standing next him with a soft smile on her face.

I follow through the crowd, making sure my mother is in my sight at all times. The music has stopped, and the overhead, even brighter lights are on. All eyes seem to be on us. If there were ever a time I would like to disappear, this would be it. I hate being the center of attention, always have. Regardless, I pull up my big girl panties and move on.

Dagger enters a room and lays my mother on a bed. The room is wood-paneled with pictures and banners draped on the walls. The bed is unkempt, and clothes are strung across the floor throughout it. Empty beer cans and bottles are on every surface. It is defiantly not the cleanest place I've ever been in before.

I move to the side of bed, kneeling down, my hip aching as I do, and grab my mother's hand gently. "Are you okay?"

She turns her head stiffly toward me, her eyes welling up, and my heart breaks for her. "It hurts a bit," she mutters through clenched teeth. I have no doubt that it does.

"I have more Vicodin in the car. You want me to go get it?" I really don't want to leave her and go through all those people outside the door, but I'll do whatever I have to do to help her.

"I'll be okay," my mother, ever the trooper, responds. Hit her with a Mack truck, and she's still just fine.

I move to get up, even though it pains me to, but she needs the medicine, even if she won't say it. "I'll be—" My words are cut off by a hand on my wrist.

My head snaps up, and I look into eyes that remind me of the ocean, but also the danger that lives beneath its surface. Rhys.

"Give me the keys. Tell me where it is, and I'll get it." My first thought is, *That's sweet.* The second thought is, *What is he playing at?* But I'm grateful for his generosity. My mother always taught me never to look a gift horse in the mouth, and I'm not starting now.

I dig in my pocket and pull out my keys. "It's in…" Oh, shit. "My purse. It's in the backseat of the car. There's a bottle inside it." I really don't want him going through my purse, not that there is anything in there of any real significance. He doesn't appear to be a respectable man who will keep his hands out of my stuff, though. *Now who's judging from the outside in, Tanner?* "Or just bring me my purse, and I'll get it."

He gives me this manly chin lift thing, snatching my keys from me, and then he's gone.

I kneel back down, my own pain settling in deep as the adrenaline I've held on to from the moment I got the call from Mom comes seeping out.

"Tell me the trouble," Dagger says, pulling up a chair and sitting down on the other side of the bed. His gaze drifts up and down my mother. For some bizarre reason, I suddenly want to cover her up.

Four other men stand around, each with their eyes trained on my mom and each with the confidence that they could end this entire situation in a second.

"You want me to?" I ask Mom, who nods slightly. "She's hurting pretty bad," I tell them like an idiot. Anyone with two eyes could see that bit of information.

I go through the entire story of what happened, not leaving a single thing out. If Mom is right, and this man or men can help us, then they may as well have all the facts.

"After cleaning Mom up, we came here."

"So the knives and clothes are in your car?" Dagger stares at me, stroking his beard up and down. It's almost like a calming thing for him, or maybe he's deep in thought.

"Yes, in a black, plastic bag. Everything is in there." I grabbed Mom's hand during the telling of the story, and she squeezed me several times in reassurance. I needed it because it's the only reason I've kept going. She is my strength.

Rhys came back in during story time, and I stopped to give Mom some more meds. Her eyes getting a bit droopy now, so she'll most likely pass out soon. That's good. She needs to rest and heal.

"Becs, Tug," Dagger says to two men in the room who were listening to every word intently. They aren't as scary as Rhys, but they are up there on the top of the pole.

"On it," one of them says as Rhys tosses my keys to them.

"Why did you give them my keys?" I ask him a little more snottily than I should have.

"Stop it," is all he says, and I glare at him. "Tanner, let the guys do their thing."

I focus back on Dagger. I hate not having any control. It may just drive me to the brink of insanity at this point. Wait, I'm already there.

"The house. You locked it up and turned off the lights?" he asks.

"Yes."

"Did you do anything else? Move him or anything?"

I cringe, thinking of his lifeless body surrounded by a pool of blood. "I didn't touch him after I figured out he was dead." Bile rises in my throat, and I choke it down.

Mom's eyes close, and the soft rise and fall of her chest tells me she's asleep. So peaceful. So unhurt.

"Good. Need the address, and I'll get it taken care of."

My eyes flip to his confident ones. "How in the world will you do that?"

"That, my dear, is none of your business. Me and the boys will handle it."

I shake my head back and forth vigorously. "Don't you get that he's a well-respected police officer there? You can't just cover it up. You can put lipstick on a pig, but it's still a pig!" My voice raises, and I instantly clamp my hand over my mouth, not wanting to wake up my mother.

"Tanner, it's taken care of," Dagger says. "Now this you-being-my daughter thing ... I'll be talking to your mother about that once I get back."

Wait. What?

"Where are you going?"

"I have to clean up this little mess. We'll roll out and be back in before ya know it."

He's going to roll out?

"You're going all the way to Tennessee?" I ask, and Dagger nods his head.

"All right, what the hell is going on now?" A beautiful woman with dark hair and red streaks comes into the room carrying a tackle box. What, is she going fishing?

"Princess, Tanner. Tanner, Princess," Dagger introduces us almost robotically.

I give a small wave with a "hi," and she does the chin lift thing. That seems to be a universal sign around here.

"Need you to look over Mearna when she wakes up and Tanner now," Dagger tells Princess.

"I'm fine," I say, instantly rising up from the floor. Dizziness assaults me, and two large hands grip my sides, holding me up and steadying me. His touch is like a fire I've never felt. It's hot, but it burns so deeply it radiates though my body. "I'm ... fine," I say on an exhale after catching my breath.

"Sure you are. I'm fine. You're fine. The world is fine. Sit in the chair and let me check you over," Princess says, coming toward me.

I have to say, she is definitely intimidating, so I listen and sit.

"Where does it hurt?" she asks, touching my arm in a spot that doesn't hurt.

I chuckle. "Probably the only place it doesn't ache is where you're touching right now."

The men in the room move off to the side and begin talking in hushed tones.

"So who won the fight?" she asks.

"He's dead, so you tell me." My eyes grow wide. I cannot believe I just said that to her. Oh, my God. A perfect stranger and I just blurted that out? Someone please shut me up.

She laughs, a full-out, throw her head back laugh. I don't know if I'm relieved or scared shitless.

"Sounds like you did, then. Need you to go in the bathroom and wash all that shit off your face. You did a pretty good job covering it all."

Without words, I do as she asks in an attached bathroom that is dirty as hell and needs to be cleaned, like, last year. Gross.

When I am done, I sit back down, and Princess moves my face this way and that, inspecting every inch of me. "Fucker got you good. Lift your shirt." I look to the guys in the room, and she follows my gaze. "Don't worry about them. They get more pussy and tits than they'll ever need." The directness of her words is like nothing I've ever heard. "What?" she asks me.

"Why do you talk like that?" Maybe I should be embarrassed, but I'm not. Shocked is more like it.

"Like what?" She waits a beat before it dawns on her. "Oh! The pussy and tits thing? Sister, if you're gonna be around these guys, you need to leave that prissy shit at the door. It won't fly here. I grew up around this. By the way, who are you?"

Prissy shit? I've never considered myself a priss before. I feel slightly offended yet say nothing.

"Apparently, I'm Dagger's daughter." Her eyes grow wide, and it feels kind of good. Something tells me she doesn't get shocked very often. "At least, that's what my mother decided to tell me a few hours ago."

"No shit?"

I feel the urge to chuckle at her puzzlement.

"No shit." I pull the T-shirt up over my head, my black bra covering all the essentials.

"Fucking hell, girl. He kicked you good."

At those words, Rhys turns to me. His gaze is so penetrating, so deep I try to cover myself up, protect myself from ... I don't know, but something. His eyes narrow as he takes in every bruise and cut on my body. He hasn't even seen the ones on my legs or back yet. I feel so exposed, naked, bare.

"Let me check. It's okay." She follows my gaze over to Rhys. "You're scaring the ever-loving shit out of her." She speaks the words I would have wanted to say.

He does some grunt thing, shakes his head, and turns back to the other guys.

Princess pokes at my ribs, and while sore, I'm pretty positive nothing is broken.

"Are you a doctor or something?"

Princess grins. "Nope, just stitched up a lot over the years. If the Doc can't get here quickly, I come in to check it out." So she has no medical training whatsoever. Great. "No worries. I watch those hospital shows on TV." She winks so I know she's joking.

I want to relax, but it's just not there. There are too many unknowns to enjoy any relaxation.

"The motherfucker you killed do that to your mom?" she asks, looking over at the bed where my mom is sleeping without a care in the world.

"Yeah. He was gonna take us both out. I didn't mean to ..." I can't lie, because if I were in that exact situation again, I wouldn't change a thing. I would have killed him. "Never mind. I did mean to. He was hurting her, and I couldn't let him do it anymore." I wait for her disgust or anger at me for taking another human's life. It doesn't come.

"Good," she says, surprising me. "Assholes like that need to be taken out."

I gape at her. I'm pretty sure I've entered a parallel universe. Since when do people talk so nonchalantly about taking another person's life? I don't even know what to say, but I cry out when she touches a spot on my side.

"You peeing blood?" she asks as I catch my breath.

"No," I grit out through my teeth. Damn, that hurt.

"Good. It's probably just bruised pretty good, but we'll have Doc take a look to make sure. You want something for the pain?"

Lord, do I want something to knock me the hell out so I can forget, but I can't, not now. This place is too different, and for my mother's sake, I need to keep my eyes open.

"Just some Ibuprofen would be nice."

"You sure you don't want some of the good stuff? I can make it so you won't feel a thing." She smiles warmly, and I have no doubt from the look on her face that she has an arsenal of feel-good pills.

"No thanks."

She nods, opening the box she laid on the floor at my feet. Inside are lots of little bottles filled with pills, and at the bottom are all kinds of medical supplies.

"Does this place have hurt people in it a lot?" The words flow out of my mouth. Where the hell is my filter?

"You'd be surprised."

I don't really think I want to know at this point. I look to my mother on the bed, the nasty bed with dirty sheets, and I'm sure the pillows are just as filthy. There's no way I can let my mom lie on that.

"I don't mean to be rude," I say as she smirks at me, giving me her full attention. "Is there any way I could get some clean bedding for my mom? That"—I point to the bed—"is just gross."

Princess laughs so hard tears begin rolling down her face, catching the attention of the guys who've been in hushed conversation. "Oh, honey." She turns to Dagger. "Dude, she doesn't even know you yet and can see you as clear as day."

"What the fuck does that mean?" Dagger glares at Princess, and I can't help the twinge of fear in that stare. Princess doesn't feel it at all as her laughter continues.

"Your sloppy self." She shakes her head, turning to

me. "I'll get some new ones." Turning to the door, she yells, "Blaze!" so loud my ears ring.

I few seconds later, the beautiful brunette who was by the entrance earlier strides through the door. "You bellowed?" Her sarcastic tone tells me these two have a pretty good relationship. I'm pretty sure there aren't many people who would talk to the woman in front of me like that.

"Can you get some clean sheets, pillow cases, blankets, the works? Dagger's room is a pit."

When Blaze smiles, it's time for me to catch my breath. That one movement lights up her face to the point beyond beautiful. "No problem. I'd change everything, too."

"Stop giving Dagger shit, or I'll turn you over my knee," the guy Dagger called Tug says, smacking Blaze on the ass with a loud thwack.

"Hey! I didn't do anything wrong," she teases, not pissed in the least. If anything, her admiring gaze tells me that she's in love with this man, deeply in love.

She kisses him on the cheek and quickly leaves the room.

"Can I get you anything?" Princess asks just as a huge guy with light hair walks in the room. I'm surprised he can get through the door.

"What's going on?" the man questions.

"Hey, babe. Two women got beaten up, one killed a guy. Oh! And this one is Dagger's kid." She points to me as shock hits the man's face. "Cruz, Tanner. Tanner, Cruz, my old man." She winks.

Damn, she did a fine job finding her a man.

"Fucking hell," he says, joining the man huddle, not really acknowledging me.

"So, what happens now?" I ask Princess.

"The boys will leave and take care of the problem. You're gonna need to answer all of their questions and not hold anything back." I nod. I've already told them the story, but I'll answer whatever they've got for me.

Holy shit, what have I gotten myself into?

4

RHYS

"FUCK, WE DO NOT NEED THIS SHIT RIGHT NOW," CRUZ SAYS as he enters the group.

He's not fucking wrong. Ravage has too much shit going on for this to happen right now. Right now, as we speak, Buzz, one of the newest brothers, is hacking some computers we got from a guy who was working with a rival club, and he's not coming up with a whole hell of a lot. We're still trying to find out who in the fuck is behind all the bullshit that's happened to Ravage these past weeks. Then I'm sure we pissed a fuck of a lot of high rollers off when we took out the motherfuckers who kidnapped Blaze, Tug's ol' lady. Now this.

"You don't think I know that shit?" Dagger snarls, going toe to toe with Cruz. "That could be my kid. If she needs protection, we give it."

I'm not too sure this whole kid thing has sunken in yet for him, but he's doing what I would do in this situation—clean it up so she doesn't feel the pain.

When she stepped into the clubhouse, it was like a magnetic force made me go to her. I had bitches lining up to fuck me, but no, I moved to her and have no fucking clue why. She's just a chick like all the rest of them. Fuck 'n' go—that's my motto. Always has been, always will be.

"Stop." Pops steps into the room, taking everything in. "Dagger, run down," he orders.

Dagger, our Sergeant at Arms, complies, his eyes swinging first to the mother on the bed then to Tanner. "Tanner," he calls to her. I don't know if he just needs to hear it or what the hell that was.

"Hi." She gives a jaunty wave, putting her hand down quickly. Just that small gesture was sexy as hell, and I'm pretty sure she has no fucking clue.

"That's Pops. He's the president around here," Princess explains to Tanner, who is quietly soaking it all in. "He's also my blood." Tanner gasps.

"Your father?"

"Yep, but we only call him Pops around here." Princess turns to Pops and winks.

"Seems like you got yourself in a mess here, Tanner." She sits quietly at Pops' words. "It seems to come with a lot of the women who enter the Ravage family these days." The last part, he practically growls. "Get Tanner a paper and pen. I need you to write down the address to the man you killed and the address of your apartment."

"Why my apartment?" she asks, taking the paper from Princess who got it off the nightstand.

"It's where you cleaned up. Blood."

I really hope we don't have to torch the apartment building. That would be way too conspicuous with the flames the mother's house, too.

"I ..." she starts then shakes her head and writes on the paper, handing it back to Princess when she is done, who gives it to Pops.

"All right. You stay here with your mom, and we'll be back." Pops turns. "Tell your ol' ladies bye; we've got shit to do." He then walks out of the room.

I don't have nor want an ol' lady. Fuck that shit. I don't want some woman barking at me this way or that. No fucking way. Regardless, something compels me to turn and look at Tanner. As I do, her face flushes as she sucks in a slight breath. At least I know I affect her. I'll fuck her, daughter or not. I need to let her heal first, though.

I lift my chin to her and leave the room.

GUNNING THE THROTTLE, I fly with my brothers up the interstate, feeling the coolness of the night around me. It's still pretty dark, but the sun will be rising soon.

I never feel as free as I do when I'm riding. I've been riding legally since I was eighteen and, illegally, a lot earlier. I started fixing up my first Harley when I was sixteen. I didn't have a fucking clue what I was doing and no money. I was just a trumped-up street kid who found a scrap of a bike and wanted to fix it up.

I had nothing, but I wanted for nothing at the same time. I stole food from local grocery stores or at restaurants. For shelter, I would find an abandoned house or take cover under the viaduct by the interstate. If I got sick, I went to the free clinic. I made do.

What I didn't have were parents. I never had a father, don't know who in the fuck he was. My mother, if you can call her that, was into so many drugs she couldn't stand half the time. Her favorite pass time was smacking me upside the head and telling me what a disappointment I was to her. Got a couple of scars to prove that because she got inventive at times and found things around our shack of a house to use instead of her hand. I was better out there. Sure, it was no roses and sunshine bullshit. It was hard, lethal, and the best fucking education a guy like me could have.

At fourteen, I knew shit about the streets. I was a puny, wimpy-ass kid named Denny Lorant who knew it would be better out there on my own than with a mother who bounced us around from place to place because she had nothing. I tried cleaning her ass up even with the shit she gave me, I did. Nothing worked with her, so I got out.

I fought a lot, got beat down a lot. I had a shit load of bones broken in my body, but with each one, I learned. I sucked in every bit of information I could and grew, not just in size, but in brains. Then, as I got older, I became the one who gave the beat downs. I was the one others feared, and I fucking loved it. It's how I got the name Rhys, because I rise above all. Some chick I knew back then came up with the spelling, and it just stuck.

When I started fixing up my first Harley, I was a flat-out sixteen-year-old punk, and I'm surprised shit happened the way it did. I consider myself one of the lucky ones. Not knowing what the fuck I was doing and only hanging around with guys who worked on cars, I started going to local garages and asking them for their help in exchange for my work in their shop, cleaning whatever the hell they wanted me to. I had the fucking door slammed in my face too many times to count.

When I came to Banner Automotive, I figured the same thing would happen: door, slam. To my surprise, it didn't. Pops introduced me to Bam who was a wiz at fixing shit. Then I was introduced to the Ravage MC, and the rest is history.

I never had a moment when I envisioned my future. Fuck no. I was lucky to survive a night out there on the streets, sleeping with one eye open all the fucking time. I never thought I would have any sort of family, but that one stop at sixteen opened my world to Ravage.

We follow Pops through a back alley and stop our bikes, killing the engines. The house is about three blocks down the way. The houses are lined up, stacked too fucking close to one another. Everyone in this fucking area will hear our bikes, so we need to play this shit cool.

It's about five a.m. on a Thursday morning; therefore, I'm sure most of these assholes will be getting up soon to head to work, which means nothing can look out of place.

"Rhys." I lift my chin to Pops, acknowledging his words. "You and Tug walk to the house and scope shit out. Come back and give us info. Then we plan." I nod as does Tug. "We're heading over to the park we passed in town. Tuck your bikes under the brush then get back to us."

We follow Pops's instructions to the T and head down the alley.

I pull a smoke out of my pocket and light it up. Nerves? What the fuck are those? I lost that shit when I went out on the streets. Fear? Nope, not there, either. This is actually fucking fun.

"This one," Tug says, pointing to the tan house with

green shutters. The entire place looks like the *Brady Bunch*—totally family-oriented.

I clip the end of my smoke with my fingers and put the butt in my pocket. No evidence gets left behind, nothing. I then slip on my black leather gloves, watching Tug do the same, and pull out my Glock from the back of my pants. We left our rags locked on the bikes, not wanting anything identifying. This is nowhere close to being a friendly meeting.

We creep up to the back door. Dried blood is covering the handle. Fuck. These women know shit for hiding stuff. My thoughts flick to Tanner. No, there is no fucking way she knows this life. She's just too ... fucking everything. I shake my head, focusing on my task.

Looking into the window, I see blood-coated footprints all over the entryway. At least they were smart enough to go out the back. Turning the handle, it opens freely, so they didn't even bother to lock the fucking door. I bite back my curse as I turn the handle and step inside the door with Tug at my back. It's been a good twelve hours, so the stench of death assaults my nostrils. Good. The fucker deserved to die.

I step around the small alcove in the kitchen where the dead motherfucker is lying on the floor in a pool of his own blood. He's a fat motherfucker. What the hell did they feed him? Well respected cop, my fucking ass. More like paid mint for all the fucking food in town. Asshole.

Blood is caked throughout the entire room. I can see by the marks exactly where Tanner and Mearna were in the room. We do a quick search of the house and find no one there, and it looks like no one else has been in the space. I do find his cell, but he doesn't have any missed calls, so hopefully no one is looking for his ass yet.

I pick up my own cell, punching in Pops' number. "Clear. Gone. Need anything?"

"No. Come to us," he says cautiously. Sure, we use burner phones, but you never know who is listening.

I have to say, I disagree with Pops here. I think we should just set the place on fire now and get the fuck out of town before everyone wakes up and gets going for the day. Instead, he wants to plan. I've never been much of a planner; I'm more of a doer.

"Now and out," I tell him, hoping he understands what I'm saying.

"Clean?" He returns, wanting to know if we can do it cleanly or if it would leave a bigger mess.

"Looks that way," I respond. The sooner we get this shit handled, the quicker we can get the fuck out of here.

"Do it," he orders.

There are not many men in this world I take orders from, but my president is one of them. Some of the brothers, possibly. Everyone else can kiss my ass. I'm relieved he sees things my way.

"On it." I click the phone off.

Tug is studying me intently, waiting for my lead. He's only been a full member of the Ravage MC for a short time, but he's a very quick learner and a man I'm happy to have at my back.

"Basement. Let's do the water heater. It's gas."

We head to the basement and blow out the pilot light of the water heater. Tug and I loosen the pipes, allowing more gas to flow through the room.

"Done," I tell him as we rush upstairs.

We check the windows, making sure all of them are closed. They are. We then move to the kitchen where Tug grabs a pot out of the cabinet, filling it halfway with water before setting it on the stove. He cranks the gas stove on high as we watch the fire come to life.

"It'll take an hour or two. Then it'll blow," Tug says.

"Then let's get the fuck out of here." The whole premises has natural gas rising, and since we shut the door to the basement, it will take a little longer to reach the fire, but by then, it will be so concentrated that ... BOOM! The entire house will explode first then catch on fire.

We head to our bikes and make our way to the park.

"Done?" Pops asks as we pull up.

"Filling with gas right now. It will blow in a couple of hours."

"How bad?" Dagger asks.

"The girls know shit about covering up a crime scene. I can only image what the fucking apartment will look like when we get there." I shake my head, pulling off my gloves. "We may need to blow the place there, too, if it looks like what we just saw."

"We can't torch it, too obvious," Pops says. "You, Dagger, GT, and Becs go over to Tanner's place and see what the hell it looks like. Then we go from there," Pops orders, grabbing the back of his neck. "I swear to Christ, you fuckers and your women are going to be the death of me."

I can see where he's coming from. First, it was Princess and the bitch who stole her and Cruz's kid.

Then, Casey, who's GT's ol' lady, when she got kidnapped. After that was Blaze who was on the run from two dickheads who raped her repeatedly. Bitches around here bring too much shit. It's why I don't get fucking involved with them—too much fucking trouble.

"Fine," I say as we head off to Tanner's place.

It's not what I expected at all after being in the newer, cookie-cutter home of her mother's. Tanner's place is two stories with four apartments in it. As we walk up the dilapidated steps to the second floor, I wonder how much she fucking pays for this shit hole of a place. I mean, fuck, the damn boards on the stairs are falling through; not to mention, the railing is wobbly as hell.

Dagger pulls out Tanner's keys and opens the door. I flip on the light, and the boys follow.

"What the fuck!" Dagger growls loudly, and I have to agree with him. The place is small, two fucking rooms small, but the size isn't what gets us. It's the cracks in the walls and the celling that is falling down with buckets underneath it to catch the water when it rains. Mold is growing on one of the walls by the kitchen sink, but despite those things, the place is immaculate. Tanner obviously takes a shit load of pride in her space, and I feel her on that shit.

I remember my first place. I was fucking ecstatic to have a fucking bed and shower. I would have dealt with all this shit, too. But why is she? I can't help the curiosity.

Dagger pushes through the space, each growl louder than the last. If I had a kid, no way in hell would I want them living like this.

"Brother," he says to me with a lost look in his eyes.

I slap his shoulder. "We'll get it figured out."

"Fuck!" he booms. "I didn't even know I had a fucking kid, and she's living like this?" As he begins to pace, I look at the other guys, hoping this shit doesn't go south, and Dagger can control his shit. "How could Mearna let her live like this?" His fists clench. He is about two seconds from punching a fucking wall.

I move up into his space, getting in his face. Dagger and I have been friends for two decades, and if anyone can handle him, it's me. "One thing at a time, brother. Let's get this shit cleaned up." Even though I see no blood, which surprises the fuck out of me, we still need to douse it in hydrogen peroxide just in case. "Then we get back and find out. No sense in losing your shit when you don't have all the facts. Got me?"

His nostrils flair, and I prepare myself for the bull that is Dagger. I might as well be wearing a fucking red shirt by the way he's looking at me.

"Snap out of it," I roar, and his eyes blink. Fucking hell. "Let's get this shit done," I order, seeming to be only one who still has a brain at the moment. The longer we're here, the more likely it is that someone will see us.

"Fuck me. Let's do this shit."

I look over to GT, who is Pops' kid and Princess's brother. He carried in the bags of peroxide from his saddlebags.

"Bathroom, kitchen," he says, heading off to wipe shit down. They say bleach kills everything, but that's not the case when it comes to blood. The only shit that makes blood untraceable is the good, old hydrogen peroxide you get in the drug store. Works every fucking time.

I move around the space. Tanner has pictures hanging on the cracked walls and a whole dresser lined with them. There are a few of just her and others of her and her mother. I see none with any friends, which seems a bit odd.

"Done yet?" I call out as Becs pulls his handy-dandy light out of his pocket. It's one of those the cops use to find traces of blood at crime scenes. He's always been excellent at it. We used to joke all the time that he would go cop on us. He's got a knack, and for us, it works like magic.

"Yep, we're good," GT calls out of the small bedroom.

"Let's go," Becs says, putting the things back in his pocket. Thank Christ.

"She kept it pretty well contained to the bathroom, and GT doused it. There was a spot on the bedroom floor, but nowhere else, not even the kitchen," Becs reports.

Tanner is smarter than I gave her credit for, or she's just a serious neat freak. Whatever. I'm ready to go home.

When we pull back up to the park, Pops sits there with a shit-eating grin on his face and Cruz and Breaker at his side.

"Done. Let's go."

I look over in the direction of the asshole's house and see smoke billowing up to the sky. Then I turn over my bike, and we head out.

At least that's one less fucking thing I have to deal with.

MY PHONE BUZZES, and I pull it out of my jeans, seeing Sandra's name on the screen. Fucking hell. A while back, this bitch went to the cops, saying she saw drugs being sold inside the clubhouse. The cops came out with a warrant on her word and completely trashed the place, destroying almost everything inside, looking for the drugs. They found nothing, but they left us with a torn up mess. I went to Sandra and persuaded her to recant her story. Yeah, I fucked her to do so, but whatever. She went back to the police station and did just that, recanted. When she did, the cops were so pissed they nailed her and threw her ass in jail for lying. She called me to bail her fucking ass out, but that shit wasn't happening. I've avoided her like the fucking plague since.

She must be out now since she's calling from her cell. I hit ignore on the screen and stuff it back in my pocket. She's called a half dozen times from jail, and if she keeps this shit up, I'll go over to her place and take her out tonight. It's on the to-do list, just not top priority. She's a fucking liability, and we can't afford to have those around here.

I GRAB the wrench before adjusting the carburetor on my bike. I went to my place after getting back last night, but noticed my bike wasn't sounding right. The first thing I did upon getting to the clubhouse was park my baby in the garage and start working. I thought about coming directly here after the trip, but with as much as Tanner crossed my mind on the drive back, I thought I would go home and get her off my mind. Too bad it didn't fucking work.

"Hey," is said softly above me, and I look up to see the most angelic face staring back down at me. Sure, there are bruises and cuts, but none of that shit diminishes her beauty.

"Hey, yourself." I toss down the wrench and rise to my feet, wiping the grease on a nearby rag.

Tanner stands with her hands in the back pockets of her jeans and flip flops on her feet. Her tight shirt has a huge mouth with a tongue sticking out, and it hugs every one of her curves to perfection. She's a small, little thing, reminding me of a little sprite. I shake my head at my thoughts.

"Dagger won't tell me anything," she says as her eyes connect to mine, almost pleading with me.

"I'm not saying shit, either. It's taken care of, and that's all you need to know." I swear I hear her growl low in her throat, and I have to admit it's pretty fucking sexy. "What are you out doing?"

She shrugs, her right shoulder hitting her ear. "I had to get out of there for a bit. I needed air." I wouldn't doubt that she does.

A phone rings, and Tanner pulls a cell from her back pocket then looks at the display. She doesn't answer, only hits ignore.

I raise my brow.

"I think it's the cops," she explains. "I'm waiting for them to leave a message so I know for sure. It's my mom's phone, actually. I've been carrying it around."

"Come on." I leave the garage, making my way over to the picnic table near the huge playset that was built for the kids. I hop up onto the table, and Tanner's hot ass follows. She sits not even a foot from me, her elbows resting on her knees. The smell of sweet flowers invades my nostrils, and I suck in deeply.

"Do you know what you're gonna say to them?" I ask.

"Yeah. Dagger won't tell me anything, but he told me to tell the cops Mom brought me down here to meet him, and we got in a car accident. I've got it; I just don't want to deal with it."

"Better sooner than later."

She nods. "It's nice here," she says softly.

"It's not bad. I grew up here, so I'm used to it."

Her head turns to me. "You have family around here?"

I stare across the compound. "The only family I've got are the brothers you see."

"I've only got my mom." She pauses, and I look at her. "She's always been my rock. It's kind of strange being hers."

"I bet, but from what I can tell, you did the right thing by coming here."

Her emerald eyes connect with mine. "I think so, but I'm shitty at this running from the law thing." She chuckles. I really like the sound.

"Yeah, you aren't good in that arena. Need to teach you a thing or two."

She shakes her head emphatically. "Nope. I don't want to know. I'm never going through this again." I wish I could tell her that it won't, but shit happens. That's life. I won't lie to her.

Her phone buzzes. "I'd better check it." She starts pushing buttons, and then her gaze goes off in the distance like she's deep in thought. She pushes the phone off and turns to me. "Yep, cops need to talk to my mother as soon as possible. I guess I should call them back."

"Might as well do it now and get it over with." I wouldn't mind listening to the conversation, either.

She shakily dials the number. "Officer Mayer?" She pauses. "This is Tanner O'Ryan, Mearna O'Ryan's daughter. You called?" She remains sitting next to me, her eyes averted.

"We were in a car accident, and Mom hasn't been feeling well; that's why I'm calling you instead of her."

"She's okay. Sore, but healing."

"Me, I'm fine. Can you tell me why you're calling?" I have to admit she's damn convincing, much better at this than her murder clean up skills.

"I understand you'd like to speak with her, but she's sleeping. I'll be more than happy to speak to you on her behalf ... Okay ... Mom brought me to Georgia to meet my father for the first time," she tells the cop, and I suck in everything on this one-sided conversation. "No, we left right after I got off work for my vacation on Thursday ... Right ... I believe she told him."

Tanner's eyes turn to me, her face white as a ghost. Guess she's finding out what happened to the house. Her jaw goes slack as she listens to the phone, her eyes searching me, but I give nothing away.

"Oh, my God. Is James all right?" That sounds pretty believable even to me. "Oh no!" she says a little bit over the top, but somehow reels herself in. "You mean he's gone? ... There's nothing left?" Her eyes grow to the size of saucers as she stares at me, silently begging me for answers. "I see ... I'll be sure to tell my mother right away ... His parents did?" I'm definitely curious about that.

"Okay. I'll tell my mom. Thank you," she says then turns off her phone.

"You guys blew up the house?" she practically squeals.

I wrap my arm around her, pulling her to my body. She's got some serious fight in her. "We did what had to be done to take care of the problem," I say in a low voice. "Do you think the cops bought the story?"

She huffs. "Seemed like it."

"Good. What's going on with his parents?"

She stills in my arms, so I release her. She wraps her hands around her body. "They claimed James's body. They are setting up the arrangements for him." She shakes her head. "We'll have to go back for that."

"It'll all work out, Sprite," I tell her, half believing it. She's the one who's got to believe it so she can keep her shit together.

She jumps off the table, brushing her ass with her hands. "I need to go and talk to my mom." She skirts away before I can say another word.

GIRLISH LAUGHTER COMES from the bar of the club, and my eyes swing to it like magnets. Tanner and Princess. From the looks of things, it's more Princess than Tanner. Her expression is kind of glum, but she's putting on a brave face. It's fake as hell, yet she's trying.

I have been away for the past day and a half on club business and haven't had the opportunity to see her since our small chat outside the garage. After hearing her conversation with the cops, I told Pops and Dagger, and all seemed well.

Looking at her now, I see exactly what I've been missing.

She's wearing these sexy as fuck jeans that curve her ass as she sits on the barstool and a navy blue shirt that hugs her just as tightly. No doubt, under those clothes is one hell of a body.

"Don't fucking think about it." Dagger comes up to the table I parked my ass at and falls in the seat beside me. "I don't have a damn clue if she's my kid or not, but if she is, stay away."

"Since when do I listen the fuck to you?" I bite back. I fucking hate people trying to control me. I'm the one in control. I keep it that way for a fucking reason. This shit isn't club-related. If I want to fuck her, I will. He may be my best friend, but even he won't tell me what to do.

"I know, but fuck." He rubs his hand over his face in frustration. "I can't believe I could have a kid. I cover that shit up religiously, but back then ..." His head shakes like he's remembering some fond memory. "Fuck, I don't know, brother."

"Don't know what to tell ya." Mearna's been knocked out on pain meds for the past couple of days while her body heals, so Dagger went with me on the run. It was good because Tanner doesn't know shit, and Dagger walking around like a caged animal is not fun.

"Why the fuck wouldn't she tell me about Tanner? My fucking kid? I've missed her whole fucking life," he drones on.

I've got to say I feel for the brother. I don't know what I would do if the tables were turned.

She's turned my way several times, our eyes connecting like some live wire between us, but neither of us have moved.

Breaker catches my eye at the bar, talking to Tanner. He's leaning against it, beer in hand, and whatever in the fuck he's saying is making her laugh. This time, it's not the fake shit I noticed a few minutes ago. No, this shit is real.

As she flips her sexy as fuck reddish-blonde hair, which I initially thought was fire red when I first saw her, but realized it was the party lights, over her shoulder, anger bubbles inside of me like hot lava. I don't know where it comes from, and I don't know why, but it's there, and it's steady. I don't like the fact that someone is making her laugh, and I don't like the fact that she's going to be leaving to go to that fuck-wad's funeral. Fuck!

The grip on my bottle gets tighter, and my breathing picks up without caution. When her head falls back from another laugh, the grip tightens, and the bottle shatters in my hand, beer spilling all over the table and shards of glass entering my hand. I know I'm cut, probably pretty badly, but my eyes don't leave Tanner. I can't even force the fuckers to.

"Brother!" Dagger yells beside me, standing swiftly and his chair scraping against the floor. "What the fuck?"

Tanner, Princess, and Breaker all look our way. Princess's eyes grow wide as she hops off the stool, grabbing a towel and darting over. Tanner quickly follows after her.

"What the hell, you big lug?" Princess says as I feel her wrapping my hand.

I need to get a fucking grip. This shit ain't right. No, I

don't do this shit. I don't care. I share all the fucking time. This has to end.

I abruptly stand, clutching the towel in my hand. "I don't need your fucking help," I bark at Princess then storm to my room.

Tanner's eyes stay on me, and I can't get the fuck out there fast enough.

5

TANNER

WHAT IN THE HELL WAS THAT LOOK HE GAVE ME WHEN HE stormed out of here? It was a mix of contentment and disgust. I know I look bad with the bruises, but I was never expecting that kind of reaction.

Before we left, I thought he may have felt whatever it is that eats at me every time he's around. Sure, it was brief, but I couldn't stay by him another minute longer since I was so damn nervous. As a result, I made the excuse that my mom needed me. Then he left with Dagger for a day or so, and now this.

"What the fuck is his problem?" Princess asks Dagger.

I realize that my mother says he's my father, but I just have issues with calling him daddy dearest right now. I don't even know the man. I don't know any of them, and they act so differently than I do.

I cornered Dagger, telling him what the cops told me, but he refused to tell me anything except what I told them was good. I didn't think it would work for shit, though. Sure, I had no one at home who was pining for me, and with my vacation, no one would be expecting me. I'm pretty much a loner, and I like it that way. However, if the house blew up, I figured there would be some investigation or something.

I tried to ask more questions, but Dagger only shook his head.

I've never had a father before, but I don't think you're supposed to be scared of him, are you? Because I'm scared as shit of Dagger. Only one person scares me more, and that's Rhys.

"Fuck if I know. Asshole got beer all over my fucking jeans," Dagger bites out. "One minute, we're talking, and the next minute, he's crushing fucking bottles with his hand."

I am probably not supposed to be totally, utterly impressed by this, but I am and also intrigued. I can't believe he's strong enough to do that. I've never met anyone who could, not that I have a lot to pick from. I have been to bars where fights break out, though. Bottles get slammed and broken on the table, but never by a fist.

"Who the hell knows with Rhys?" Princess says, shaking her head. "I swear that man is going to combust one day."

"Why do you think that?" I question. I mean, there has to be a reason one would think that way.

"He's not one to mess with, Tanner. He's hard. Biker hard."

I stare at her, stunned. "What in the hell is biker hard?"

Princess motions for me to come back over to the bar. I follow and jump up on the stool. "Biker hard ..." She sits there in seriously deep contemplation.

"Is it that hard to describe?"

"For me, kinda. I've grown up in this life; it's all I know. Someone from the outside more than likely won't see things the way we do. It's hard to explain." Princess grabs her beer and takes a long pull from it.

I say nothing, because what can I say? I have no idea, and if she can't explain it when she's lived it, how in the hell am I going to figure it out?

"Let's do an easy one." Princess points to the corner of the room, my eyes following her finger. "What do you see?"

"Uh ... Three women sitting on the couch with practically no clothes on." Well, really, no clothes. What they have are small scraps of fabric that cover their nipples and other lady parts. Damn, I would never wear something like that out in public and around all these guys.

"Those are club mommas."

I turn back to her. "Club mommas?"

"Yep. Free pussy." I gasp at the thought. "They give it up to whomever, whenever, and however. Any brother, that is."

"They do what?" I pause. "Like prostitutes?" I've never been around one. Sure, I've seen movies and seen it depicted on television, but never actually met one. I'm not a prude by any means, but really?

"No, not prostitutes. Those girls don't get paid."

"Then why do they do it?" At least get paid for it.

"To be part of the club. They aren't really, but it's the closest they are ever going to get. They put their pussy out there for all the guys, so they get a spot on that couch and protection, but if they bring any bad shit to the club, they're out," Princess explains.

"Is that what you are?"

Princess sucks in a deep breath and waves pulsate off her. I immediately feel like a heel. Me and my stupid big mouth.

Dagger chuckles. "Nope, Princess won't give up that pretty pussy to anyone but Cruz. It's a damn shame." I still at his words, and Princess must see it.

"You're freaking your kid out, Dagger," she tells him, shaking her head, but a smile graces her face.

"I am who I am, Princess." And I'm totally getting that vibe from him. It seems like every man here is who he is and makes no changes for anyone. *Okay, Tanner, welcome to biker world.*

"No, Tanner, I'm not a club momma. I'm an ol' lady." I really need to brush up on this shit, because if I ever called my mother an old lady, she would tan my hide.

"I need another beer," Princess murmurs before going to get one and coming back. "An ol' lady is one of the brothers' women." She turns around, showing me the back of her leather vest. It says '*Property of Cruz.*'

"Property?" I question.

"Yep. I'm his. In our relationship, it also means that he's mine. We are committed to one another and no one else. He doesn't screw around with other women, and I don't screw around with other men. It's like marriage, biker style." She twirls the bottle as I take in the information, my mind racing at all the thoughts circling it, starting to put the pieces together. "I only wear this when I'm here at the club with the brothers or with my man. There are rules to wearing it."

"So some 'brothers' "—I kind of stumble on that word a bit—"have ol' ladies and still have other women?"

"Yep. If both parties agree to the scenario, then that's what it is."

I again try to wrap my head around this information. I guess it wouldn't be cheating if they both agree to it, but who would? Who would allow their significant other to be with someone else? I look over to the women still sitting on the couch. I could never allow my guy to do that shit to me. It's not even on my radar.

"I'm sure I couldn't do that. So how does that work? With you and them here in the same space?"

"It gets tricky at times, especially if one of the brothers is getting it on the side, and the ol' lady doesn't know. One thing you gotta know about the club is that the club and brothers come first. It doesn't matter what situation it is; those two things are always first."

It seems very stonage-ish, but I keep that to myself. Who the hell am I to say anything? I have no clue. I have no reason to judge. If this is my father's life, then it is. It also doesn't mean that my mother and I need to be part of it.

"It's just a lot to take in."

Princess laughs. "You have no idea, sister."

Sister? Did she really just call me that? Warmth comes to my heart. I've never had a sister before, and just being called that is ... well, awesome.

"Sister?" I question.

"Around here, us ol' ladies or kids of brothers, we're family. We call each other sisters. It's an endearment between us."

I smile at that. I have only ever had my mom. I had a couple of good friends, but they are long gone, living their lives. I haven't talked to them in ages. Sure, I have my co-workers, but that's exactly what they are—people I work with. I wouldn't exactly call them friends.

I always wondered what it would be like to have an actual family, one you would spend holidays with or have big meals with. Don't get me wrong, my mom did the best she could, and I do not begrudge her one bit for that. It is merely something that I have never experienced before, and I gotta admit I like it, maybe even more than I should. I'm also confounded because I don't exactly know how to act with it.

"I'd better go check on my mom." I hop off the stool and begin my way to Dagger's room.

Mom's been pretty out of it, and I know Dagger wants to talk to her, but that just hasn't been an option yet. Hell, I would like some answers, too.

I've been sleeping with Mom, so I'm grateful to Blaze for getting those clean sheets. I even scrubbed Dagger's bathroom yesterday, too scared to sit on it to pee.

"Fuck!" is yelled through one of the doors as I make my way down. I stop at the semi tortured sound. "Son of a motherfucker." This time, it's growled in pure pain. Rhys.

Should I knock? Should I keep on walking? Shit. He may have something up his ass, but I know the guy who talked to me yesterday is in there.

I knock softly and push open the door, poking my head in. "Rhys?"

His eyes snap to mine, fury pulsing off his body in waves so thick I'm surprised I'm still upright and not falling on my ass.

"Did I say you could come in?" he barks, and I jump at his unexpected words.

"I—"

"No. I didn't fucking say you could come in here."

I'm so stunned by his harsh tone that I don't know what to do. My feet are stuck to the floor. Do I stay? Do I go? I'm not sure which. And why in the hell is he so pissed off?

"I heard you yelling and thought I could help. Sorry." I start to shut the door, realizing I need to get the hell out of here. Thankfully, my feet are finally listening to my brain.

"Stop," he barks, and once again, my body listens, halting in its tracks. "Shut the door and come here."

Before I can think, I'm standing in front of him by his desk where he sits with his bloodied hand wrapped in a towel, the redness seeping through the fabric.

"Can you get the glass out?" he asks me.

Again, I don't even think, only move on instinct, grabbing the small tweezers on the desk and pulling the lamp closer to his hand to see better.

"You gonna move the towel?" I ask, ready to examine his hand.

He grunts, setting it to the side.

The gash from the glass is deep, red, and a bit puffy. The blood has slowed to only a trickle since he held the towel for compression. However, small shards of glass reflect in the light.

Rhys says nothing, but grabs a bottle of amber liquid from the floor beneath him, taking a hard pull on it then setting it back down.

Carefully, I remove each small piece I see while Rhys doesn't even flinch or move an inch. This has to hurt in some way. Even when I pull out a larger chunk of glass, no reaction comes from him. He sits there stoically, unmoving, unyielding. I can't help being impressed by his strength.

"Does it hurt?" I ask carefully, trying to gauge how he's feeling and not doing a great job of it.

"Doesn't feel good," he remarks, picking up the bottle and taking another swig.

I pull out the last shard and look up at him. "You should really get it cleaned out and stitched up."

My mouth gapes open as Rhys takes the bottle of liquor and pours it directly on the cut. Again, he acts as if he poured water on it, and it doesn't burn in the slightest. He doesn't move, simply pulls the bottle back up to his lips and drinks.

"Clean," he comments.

I close my mouth, gathering my thoughts because, at the moment, they are all over the place: confusion of his anger, admiration for his strength, lust for his body, and so many more that I can't put my finger on.

"Stiches?" He sets his bottle down and throws me a small bottle of liquid stiches.

"All righty then," I mummer, opening the bottle. I've used these before; there isn't anything to them.

I reach over to a box of Kleenexes, pull some out, and dab his wounds, getting the liquid off. I then begin to place the clear liquid on the wound.

"Why did you do this to yourself?" I ask, pulling the skin together to seal the cut and then holding it taut.

Rhys takes another drink. If I had drunk as much as him, I would be drunk as hell right now. A cold shiver goes down my spine from remembering the last time that I was in the presence of a drunk, and my hands still.

"What?" he asks, startling me from my thoughts.

"Nothing," I answer quickly, needing to get this over with then get the hell out of here and to my mother. Rhys still scares me, and having him drunk, my gut tells me, is not a good situation.

Rhys sets the bottle down as I hold his cut together, letting the stitches do their job. His other hand comes to my chin as he lifts my head, and my eyes fly to his.

"You don't lie to me, Sprite. Ever." The seriousness in his tone and eyes floors me. I feel compelled to listen to him, and I have no idea why.

I give a soft nod. I also can't help the pang that rushes through me at the name sprite, another something confusing.

"What were you thinking about?" he asks.

When I pull my bottom lip into my mouth and try to think of how to put this, his thumb comes to my lip, pulling it away from my teeth. I open my lips, my tongue darting out to touch the top of his finger automatically. He tastes of man and salt.

Rhys growls low and deep as my pulse begins thumping rapidly in my veins. What is going on here? Who am I kidding? I know exactly what is going on. My body is responding to this scary as hell man who could be old enough to be my father.

"You're drinking a lot," I finally answer. "Last time I was with someone drunk, it didn't end so well."

"I'm nowhere near drunk," he tells me, and I can't stop the uncertainty, so I divert.

"How long have you known Dagger?"

He quirks his brow as I work. "Nice change." He catches me. "I've known him about twenty years."

"And that makes you how old?" I'm digging. I admit it.

I want to know more about this man. He intrigues me like no other. I sort of get the biker hard from the outside, but is it on the inside, too? Just from our brief conversations, I've only learned he has no family, sort of like me. Somehow, I feel that connects us.

"Forty-four."

I think for long moments, trying to decide how I feel about it. On one hand, society would have a field day with it, but I'm not society. I can't worry about what others will think, but the one I am concerned about is my mother. Listen to me, already thinking ahead when I have no idea what's even in front of me.

"What?" he asks.

"You're twenty-one years older than me," I tell him, something he already knows. "How old is Dagger?"

"Fifty-one." My eyes widen as I do the math in my head. My mother is forty-one, so that makes my father ten years older than her. Wow. I let that sink in for a moment. When my mother said she was young when she hooked up with my father, I didn't realize he was that much older.

I snap out of my thoughts, finish up his hand, and then sit back on my heels, looking up at him.

"You gonna talk or let me guess what's going on in the pretty head of yours?"

He said pretty. I bite my lip. "Just doing the math on ages."

"Does the age thing bother you?"

That is a very loaded question. I think I'm a little stunned more than bothered.

I shrug. "It's my mother and Dagger's life," I finally

say, because that fact is true. I can't be the judge of any of that.

"I meant that I'm twenty-one years older than you."

My eyes widen just as the air in the room starts crackling with a charge between us. Some invisible connection between the two of us flairs to life, and my breathing picks up as I feel it deep in my bones.

Rhys eyes me. "Fuck it," he grinds out.

His hand on my chin leaves me and is placed behind my head. He pulls me to him, his lips touching mine. I take that back. His lips don't touch mine; his lips devour mine. I've been kissed, but this isn't kissing. What Rhys is doing to me is all-consuming, sucking every bit of breath out of me and leaving me so wanton I fall into it. His lips move with the precision of years of practice, knowing each movement with ease. They are soft yet demanding as he plunges his tongue in my mouth, taking everything I give and then taking more.

I wrap my arms around his hard body as he stands from the chair, pulling us together. Each plane of his defined body touches some part of mine. His hands move to my arms, pulling them away from him. I follow willingly, too involved with the kiss to give anything a second thought. All I can think of is him and the fire burning inside me.

He clutches my wrists in one of his big hands behind my back, subduing me. His other hand comes to my face, the warmth of it seeping into my blood.

He abruptly pulls away, and my wanting lips try to follow his to get them back, to get the glorious feeling that he gave me back.

"I'm going to tie you to my bed and fuck you all damn

night." The deep baritone of his voice, combined with the words he spoke, set off a fire so hot inside that it inflames me.

I have never been tied up, never thought I would want to be, but in this moment, I'm pretty sure I would do anything he said.

Rhys studies me intently. "Fuck. Your pupils are dilated and cheeks are pink. You fucking like it." He doesn't give me a second to answer as he collides his lips to mine again, taking me in a punishing, brutal, delectable kiss.

"Tanner!" Dagger's voice booms through the closed door just as Rhys pulls back in a huff.

"Fuck," Rhys growls. "In here!" he calls to the door as it swings open.

Dagger's eyes scan me up and down, and I turn my head from his stare. I don't feel bad about what I did, but he's my father, and that has to be weird or something. Hell, I don't know. My head and body are still so wrapped up in Rhys that I can't think.

"Fucking hell, Rhys," Dagger says in an annoyed tone.

"What do you fucking want?" Rhys growls, his hand still restraining mine.

I pull, trying to get away, but he only tightens his grip, so I look up at him.

"Stay," is all he says to me, and I blink my eyes rapidly.

Did he just tell me to stay like some fucking dog? The fog he put me under starts to evaporate as anger replaces it.

"Let me go." I give him my fuck-off voice and tug on my arms again.

"No," he says then turns his attention back to Dagger. "What?"

"Brother, let her go." The air in the room changes, becoming thick and dense. It's coming off both Rhys and Dagger like a bulky smoke.

I suck in a deep breath, knowing I'll only add fuel to this fire if I don't tread carefully.

"Rhys," I call, getting his attention back. "Please let me go. I have to go check on my mom." I say it calmly, trying to defuse the bomb that I feel may go off at any moment.

"That's why I came to find you. She's awake and demanding she see you." Dagger shakes his head from side to side. "She hasn't changed a bit."

There is so much I want to know to this story, but one situation at a time.

"See? I have to go," I tell Rhys, whose eyes are pissed as hell and brows drawn together.

After what feels like the longest stare down in my life, he releases my hands, and I pull them in front of me then begin to rub my wrists, hoping he didn't leave marks on my body. I already have enough of those.

I step back a few feet, giving us some distance. "Hope you feel better," I tell him, still rubbing the sensitive skin as I turn to Dagger. "I'm going to her."

I dart from the room so fast one would think my ass is on fire, but I don't care. I need time to process all of this.

6

TANNER

I RUSH INTO DAGGER'S ROOM TO FIND THE BED IS EMPTY, and my stomach plummets.

"Mom?" I yell, concern and fear cutting through me like a sharp knife.

The door to the bathroom opens, and my mother appears with Princess holding her up.

"There you are." Her voice is filled with pain. I would do anything to fix that for her.

I move quickly to her side.

"She had to pee while waiting for you, so I took her," Princess says, sitting Mom down on the bed gently.

I help her get comfortable on the bed, moving the pillows and pulling up the blankets to cover her body.

"Thanks," I tell Princess, so happy she was here to help my mom.

"Looks like you were busy." Princess chuckles.

My eyes flash to hers, my hands moving to my lips. They feel full and puffy. I shake my head, hoping she understands me. My mother is lying here, hurt, and there is no reason to bring anything else on the table right now.

"How are you feeling?" I ask Mom, focusing on her. Her brows are tight, and with only slivers of her eyes available to see, I can't read her fully.

"Like I got beaten up." She gives a soft chuckle then immediately begins coughing from it.

I sit on the bed, instantly feeling like the adult to her as the child. I grab her hand. "Mom, breathe for me. Slow and steady. In and out." I mimic what I want her to do, and she begins following. Just by holding her hand, I can feel her body begin to relax.

"Want me to give her something?" Princess asks, angling her head to her tackle box of meds.

I nod my head, not wanting my mom to feel any pain at all. Ever.

"Mom, what hurts the worst?" When the doctor came and checked her out while the boys were gone, he said that nothing was broken, but it would take her a while to heal. I'm also supposed to call him once she is lucid enough to answer questions. I need to remember to do that.

"My ribs and chest." Her breath comes out a bit wheezy.

"Your ribs are bruised bad, but not broken. The doctor said it'll take a while for it to feel better."

My mother turns her head to Princess. "Are you the doctor?"

Princess smiles. "No. I'm Princess, Pops and Ma's daughter."

Mom tries to widen her eyes, but comes up short and

moans in pain, instead. "Really?" she asks through her busted lip.

"Yep. Got a brother, GT. He's around here some-where." Princess rifles through her box. "So, you and Dagger?" she asks.

My mother turns her head. "Yes," is her only response, and this time, the ache in her voice is not from the physical pain she's in. This is deeper. She sucks in a breath. "How's Ma doing?" She changes the subject.

"Great. She's with Cooper, my little boy, right now. She's been by a couple of times while you were out."

Mom gazes off. "She probably thinks the worst of me. Hell, I bet everyone in this club does at this point." A lonely tear falls from the corner of her eye.

"Mom, they've all been great. You were right; I don't know what they did, but Dagger took care of everything. We just need to get you better." I brush the hair away from my mother's face.

"But I need questions answered." I jump at the deep voice of Dagger, who strides through the room and stops at the side of the bed.

My mother's grip tightens on my hand, and I try to get a little bit of reprieve by pulling back, but it doesn't help. It's not fear, though. She's not scared, but I can also tell she doesn't want me to leave her, and I won't.

"Here," Princess says, breaking up the tension that has seemed to enter the air. She hands me a bottle with pills. "These will help her. Two every four hours, no more. They're strong as hell, so they'll keep her knocked out, but it's the best thing for her while her body heals up."

I take the bottle. "Thanks." I set it on the bed next to me.

"I'm heading out. Call Doc," Princess addresses me and I nod. "He'll need to do whatever it is he does and make sure she's good, but from the looks of it, she'll be fine."

"Thank you." I feel like all I've done with Princess is thank her repeatedly, but she's helped my mom out so much, so what else can I do?

Once she gives me a soft smile and leaves the room, Dagger pulls up a chair, moving it close to the bed and me. Is it unusual to feel this uneasy with your long-lost father? I hope so because it's there, and it sucks.

"Mearna, tell me," Dagger presses.

I would really like to hear this myself. What she told me in the car had to be the short version of it. So much more seems to have gone on here.

"I found out I was pregnant after I left, Cameron." She closes her eyes and breathes out. "I mean Dagger."

"And you're sure she's mine?" he asks, causing my back to stiffen.

My mother opens her eyes and narrows them at Dagger. "What do you think? Think long and hard about your answer." He takes a bit, and Mom doesn't let it rest. "You want a paternity test to prove it? Fine, do it. But you know she's yours. I never messed around on you, and after I had her, I wasn't with anyone for over three years." That piece of information surprises me, but when I think back, I don't remember ever seeing my mother with anyone, not that I would remember at that age. It was just me and her, and we were happy with that.

Something flashes in Dagger's eyes then dissipates.

"You didn't think to tell me?" Dagger presses, the gruffness in his voice changing from questioning to pissed, but his body stays pretty relaxed, given the topic of conversation.

"No," my mother answers evenly. "I wasn't going to tell you."

"Why, because of the club?" Dagger's voice rises.

"You didn't love me, Cam—Dagger. I had already decided to leave. There was no need for you to know." Mom shuts her eyes like the memories are too powerful to bear.

"You're dead fucking wrong. I loved you, so don't you dare throw that shit at me."

I suddenly feel like I shouldn't be here for this intimate conversation. I feel like the odd man out, but my mother's steel grip on my hand tells me I'm not going anywhere.

"Second, you know, if I knew I had a kid, I'd want to be a part of her life."

That statement hurts a bit, but I suck it down. I always wondered whether my father would have wanted to be a father to me or if he would have ignored me if he had known about me. I'm not sure how I feel about the answer he gave, though. Part of me aches for all the time I've missed getting to know him and the other part is so confused.

"What, Dagger? Going to bring her to club parties? Drink with your friends? Come on." My mother's annoyed voice catches me off guard. Hell, she doesn't have enough strength to get to the bathroom by herself, let alone go toe to toe with Dagger.

"Bullshit. This isn't on me, Mear. *You* did this shit. You

fucking hid my kid from me." Dagger's fists clench, and I go into protective mode, immediately moving closer to my mother.

His eyes flash to mine in recognition of my stance. "I'd never lay a hand on her. Even though I'm pissed as shit that she kept you from me, I'd never hurt her." He turns back to my mother who nods. I relax a little yet stay on guard.

"It was the best decision, Dagger. You have to admit it."

"Bullshit. You didn't tell me, because you didn't want to come back. You wanted to stay away from me; that's why you didn't tell me. You knew that, if I knew about the baby, I'd have taken care of you, and you would have been stuck here with me. You wanted out, so don't try this holier-than-thou bullshit on me. It doesn't work." Dagger's tone is clipped, making my heart break for my mother. She still loves this man, and I have no doubt that what he says is one hundred percent true from the way my mother's acting. How differently would my life have been?

My mother turns her head away from us, the sound of a sniffle entering the room.

"Okay," I say, breaking this up. She's been through too much, and this is not helping the situation. "I need to give Mom her medicine and check her bandages. Can you give her a break?" I ask him—well, more like demand, but he doesn't seem like the type of guy who takes to demands very well.

"Mearna, this shit is not done." Dagger stands from the chair just as the door to the room flies open, all of our eyes moving to the sound.

"Dagger!" a light-brown-haired woman shrieks. "Where in the hell have you been?" she says to him.

The woman is wearing a leather vest like the one Princess wears, but it's her pissed off face that grabs my attention.

"Flash, get the fuck out of here." Dagger's tone is impassive.

My eyes widen as Rhys moves in the door behind the woman, his eyes intent on me then on the woman.

"You haven't even checked in. You always check in so I know you're not dead." The woman puts her hand on her hip, jutting it out in a bitch stance.

My mother's hand begins to tremble.

"I don't gotta do nothing. Get the fuck out."

"Who the fuck is this?" The woman's eyes come to me and my mother, her anger radiating off her. "This your piece on the side?" I want to punch the fucking woman. Can she not see how badly my mother is beaten? What the hell is wrong with her? I rise from the bed, my mother still clutching me.

"I'm no piece of anything," I say as her eyes pierce into mine.

"I didn't ask you shit, you stupid bitch," the woman growls, and my spine straightens.

"Enough!" Dagger barks out.

Rhys comes up behind me, his hand resting on my shoulder, and I feel instant comfort.

"Bullshit, enough. That bitch talks to me, and I get the enough?" the woman—Flash is it?—doesn't want to give up.

Dagger moves quickly, grabbing the woman and

pushing her up against the wall of the room with his forearm.

I jump as fear takes me over. What the hell is he doing? He said he wouldn't hurt my mother, but he'll hurt this woman?

"See that girl standing there?"

Flash nods her head, her eyes wide as Dagger points to me.

"That's my daughter."

"What?" Flash says in a gasp of disbelief, but Dagger doesn't answer.

"That woman in the bed is the mother of my child. Now you know what the fuck is going on." Dagger steps away from Flash, but she stays by the wall, stunned. Dagger turns to me. "Give your mom the medicine."

My shoulders jump, and I listen to what he says, helping my mother sit up and take the pills while the room stays silent.

"You have a kid?" Flash asks.

"Looks like it," Dagger answers.

Rhys stands there, almost feeling like a bodyguard of some sort, but surely Flash wouldn't come after my mother or myself, would she?

"But ..."

"No more questions!" Dagger yells, and my mother moans.

"Cameron, stop yelling," she says quietly.

Flash sucks in a breath so deep it takes all the oxygen from the room. Then her eyes widen and go to Dagger. "Cameron?" she whispers, shaking her head. "No one ..." She trails off.

"No, and don't fucking start."

"What's your name?" Flash asks my mother.

"None of your fucking business. Get out," Dagger orders.

"Mearna," my mom answers softly.

"Fucking shit," Flash whispers, looks at Dagger, and then leaves the room in a rush. What the hell is that about?

I turn my attention back to Mom, whose eyes are starting to glaze over. "Mom, you okay?"

"Tired," she answers, shutting her eyes. It takes seconds before her breathing evens out, and then she is completely out of it. Thank God.

"Let's let her rest," I tell Dagger and Rhys. Dagger looks at my mom, turns, and then leaves the room. "Go ahead, Rhys. I'm going to lie with her for a while."

His eyes pierce mine, holding me in place. I don't know what it is about this man, but something pulls me, and it's scaring the shit out of me.

"An hour. Then I'm coming to get you."

I try to refute his statement, but before I get one word out, he's gone, shutting the door behind him.

I kick off my shoes and carefully lie on the queen-sized bed next to my mother, being extra careful not to touch her. I lie on my back and stare at the brown, stained ceiling.

What in the hell am I going to do? Mom and I need money. What she brought won't sustain us for long. I need for Mom to get better first, though. That has to be the goal right now. Get Mom well, and then I'll figure out where we can go and what we need to do. Everything is so up in the air right now, and I need to simply relax and let the cards lay, at least for now. In a couple of days, when Mom can stay awake for more than a few hours, we'll talk and figure it out.

I can't believe I have a father. Well, I'm not stupid. I knew I had one, but you get the point. Seeing him manhandle Flash was scary as hell. It reminded me of James and the way he treated my mother. I did see a difference, though, because Dagger told the woman to leave, and she wouldn't listen, whereas James did it for the hell of it. It still scares me. Maybe that's why my mom left him, but if that's the reason, then why in the hell did she stay with James? That's the part I just don't get. Hopefully, she'll be able to enlighten me when her body heals a bit since the questions keep piling up.

These past few days have worn on me. I haven't slept much with trying to make sure my mom was all right and then worrying about when the boys were coming back and what they did.

I allow my body to relax as I roll to my side and stare at my mom, watching her chest rise and fall softly. I allow the sounds to lull me to sleep.

I WAKE WITH A JOLT. I look around my surroundings, quickly putting together that I'm in Dagger's room. My mother is passed out next to me as the soft hum of music beats through the door.

I wipe my face, get up, and use the bathroom. Looking in the mirror, I wince at the purple and yellow marks on my face. Not that I'm trying to impress anyone, but why in the hell did Rhys kiss me when I look like this? I shake my head. Just the thought of his kiss has my head spinning. Was that just a kiss?

My mother's moans pull me out of my thoughts as I move swiftly to the bed. She is tossing, no doubt hurting herself even more than needed. Reluctantly, I hold her shoulders so she can't turn.

"Mom, wake up," I tell her, feeling her muscles bunch under me. "Mom!" I say a little more loudly, and her eyes flutter open.

"What?" she groans, her eyes half-lidded. Her body settles down, and I remove my hands.

"Are you awake?" I ask, needing to know if I'm talking to her or if she's sleep talking. When I was younger, my mother talked in her sleep all the time. I used to think it was hilarious. Now, not so much.

"Yes." Her voice is scratchy and hoarse. "I need something to drink." She pauses. "Something warm."

I brush her hair away from her beautiful face, noting it looks so much worse than mine does. "I'll get you something. Maybe they have some soup or something. You really need to eat." I've been forcing her to drink, keeping fluids down her since she refused to eat in the small bouts that she's awake, but it's time. She needs to try something.

" 'Kay," she says, her eyes fluttering shut. I'll have to wake her when I get back.

Since being here, Princess has showed me around the kitchen and pantry. This place keeps enough food on hand to feed an army. I still feel leery of just helping myself to whatever we need, but Princess been nothing but kind to me, and she's definitely a straight talker. If it was a problem that we ate here, I'm sure she would be one of the first people to say something.

I follow the hallway lined with pictures and different plaques. With each step, the music gets a little louder. Entering the main room of the clubhouse, I see people are scattered everywhere. Some of the brothers I met before are among some others I have not. Rhys sits with his back to me, arm extended over the empty chair next to him, the cord of his muscles flexing and bunching. In the other hand, he has a beer, and he's talking to Cruz, who sits next to him.

I gaze over to the corner of the room where the back of my father is to me. He's standing in front of a couch, and a woman's hands are wrapped around his thighs. His hips are moving back and forth, and I pause in step. Holy shit is he ...? Shock fills me at the sight. Please tell me that I'm not seeing my father, the father I just met, get his penis sucked by one of those club mommas Princess told me about. This is seriously not happening.

I force my feet to move toward the kitchen, my eyes glued to my father. However, once I see the confirmation of what I thought is happening, I jerk my head straight ahead. He is, right in the middle of the club, with people around him. I ... My thoughts skip as I force myself into the large pantry where the food is stacked and search for some type of soup.

I suck in deeply and bow my head. I can't believe I just saw that. No child should ever have to see that, new father or not.

Hands grip my shoulders so I can't move, and I scream loudly enough to wake the dead.

"Shh ..." Rhys's deep voice trembles in my ear, but my

breathing doesn't slow. This time, it is amped up by his baritone voice and light breath. His hands release me and move up and down my arm. "You all right?"

I nod my head, trying to get myself under control.

He pulls me flush to his hard body, and I close my eyes, enjoying the feel of him. Each sweep of his fingers on my flesh sends my body into a state of arousal that is so over the top I'm not sure how to come down or even if I want to. Not only that, but it's comforting and secure. How this man can pull off these feelings inside me is insane. I should be running for the hills, but I can't, don't want to.

"Saw a show out there?" The fizzle I felt starts to fade as the images that I don't want to see come back. I shiver.

He chuckles, which seems so strange for him that I turn around, seeing a small smirk on his face. I'm taken aback by it because that small change in his face completely transforms him, almost creating a whole different person. How is that possible? How can one expression turn him totally around from mean, scary, and sexy to sinful, amused, and drop-dead gorgeous? It's like he's two different people.

He doesn't allow me to process these thoughts. Instead, the smirk disappears, and heat sparks in his gaze as he crashes his lips to mine, taking my breath away for the second time tonight.

The cut on my lip has healed enough that there is no pain, but with each movement of his lips, I feel him snag a piece of the skin. It only heightens the pleasure in the kiss.

Rhys shifts, wrapping his steel-banded arms around

me, not leaving an inch between our bodies. I'm so lost in the kiss it's the only thing I can focus on.

"Dammit." Dagger's voice from the doorway echoes through the small space.

I pull away, feeling like a teenager getting caught by her father. Oh, wait, everything in that scenario is right except for the teenager part.

Rhys growls, obviously pissed for the second interruption from Dagger. I'm not sure if I am or not, but one thing is for sure, father or not, he's going to see the real Tanner O'Ryan.

7

RHYS

I'M SURPRISED I CAN'T SEE THE STEAM COMING OUT OF Tanner's ears at this point. Her body is so fucking tight, and from the way she clenches and unclenches her hands, she is itching to take out some frustrations. By the look of it, on Dagger.

Sure, seeing your father getting sucked off by some random momma will leave someone not in the life a bit pissed off. But if she goes off halfcocked, she'll realize quickly who her father really is, and that would fuck with both of them.

I know I shouldn't care, but the weird thing is, I do. I actually care that they are about to fuck up their relationship before it starts.

"You," she growls, turning in my arms to face Dagger.

I tighten my grip on her, feeling in my gut that she's planning on lunging at any time. I won't allow that, but stopping her mouth is another obstacle.

"What?" Dagger shrugs, crossing his arms over his chest.

Dagger is who he is. No one, not even his little girl, is going to change that shit. I've been with him here in the club for twenty something years. Dagger is Dagger. She's gonna have to learn the true him if she wants any part of him in her life.

"How could you just get your ...?" Tanner trails off, swallowing deep, then resumes. "Penis sucked in front of a group of guys?" Her arms flail in the air as she speaks. "I don't know what's worse: you getting a blow job in front of a group of men or the fact that it was such a normal thing not one person even gave you a second glance." Tanner huffs as she tries to pull away from me, but I refuse to let her go.

"I needed to get off, and that's what they're here for," Dagger says, only infuriating Tanner more.

"No wonder my mother wanted to get me away from here, away from *you*," she spits out. For once in his life, Dagger looks as if Tanner just smacked him across the face with a two-by-four. I never thought I would see the day that happened. "Having sex in public while people watch, not caring one bit ... She knew she was better than this garbage."

Dagger goes from shocked to pissed in a nanosecond, taking a step closer. Fuck.

"Listen here. I would have given your mother—"

"What?" Tanner jumps in. "Just like you have that Flash chick? Is she your wife, and you just come here to get your rocks off?" Tanner's fingernails bite into the skin of my forearm, but I don't release her. That would be one of the worst things I could do at this moment.

I take a step back, putting the two out of arm's reach.

"I'm a grown-ass man; I'll do what the hell I want,

when I want. You or anyone else is gonna tell me any different," Dagger shoots back, pointing to his chest.

"I'm not telling you what to do. I just can't believe my mother still loves you after knowing all of this." Tanner's arm flies out as she waves her arm, motioning to the clubhouse.

"Your mother almost married a man who beat the shit out of her. I never touched a hair on that woman's head out of anger," Dagger fires back.

"She never said you did. Hell, I didn't even know you existed."

"Sugar, that street goes both ways."

Tanner lets out a huge, long breath, the muscles in her body losing some of the starch. "Look, I need to get my mom to eat something. The sooner I get her better, the sooner we'll be gone and out of your hair." She grabs my arm again. "Let me go."

I step back as she grabs the can from the shelf, turns her back, and strides out into the main kitchen.

"Fuck me," Dagger says, running his hand over his face. "Never in a million years seen this coming. Shit, she's a firecracker." He shakes his head in silent reflection. "Should have known. Mearna's one, too." Dagger looks almost glum, and that is not like him one bit.

"You wanna talk about it?" I ask.

"Nah, I'm good." He runs his hand over his neck. "Gotta head out for a bit. Need to ride." He leaves hastily. That's typical Dagger, though. When shit gets tough, he rides it out. He'll come back better.

I stride into the kitchen, locating Tanner quickly as she sticks a bowl in the microwave, pushing the buttons to turn it on. She looks over at me, frustration written all over her face, then drops her head.

"I shouldn't have yelled at him." She shakes her head, her arms resting on the counter to hold up the weight of her body. "I don't even know the man. Why do I care?"

"Well, you care because he's your father. All the other shit, you're gonna need to talk to Princess or one of the other ol' ladies about."

Her head rises just as the buzzer beeps on the microwave. She pulls it out and steps away. "I need to go help my mom."

I want to grab her arm as she leaves, but I'm not a dick enough to want to her hurt by the hot liquid that could spill if I do.

I told her earlier an hour, but when I went in to get her, she was sleeping so fucking peaceful next to her mother I didn't wake her. The worry that she seems to carry around with her all the time had been wiped from her face.

The way she takes care of her mother, not having one selfish act with her, is unbelievable. I never had another human being give a shit about me until I joined Ravage, and the fact that Tanner gives with her whole heart … I shake my head.

I let her sleep before, but now I'll give her thirty minutes to get her mother sorted, and then I'm going in after her.

I grab a beer and sidle up to the bar, taking a long swig and lighting a smoke. Breaker comes through, giving me a chin lift and walking to the pantry to grab food.

"What's going on?" I ask.

"Buzz. He's getting close to cracking the computer, so I'm getting him something to keep him going."

I lift my chin in response and take a pull from the bottle.

A strong hand clamps on my shoulder. "How's it going?" Pops asks with a wide smile.

I'll never forget what Pops did for me all those years ago—taking in a punk kid who had nothing and giving him more than he ever thought possible.

"Fine." And it is for the most part. My dick is hard as a rock, but other than that, nothing big.

"Chasing tail?" Pops asks with a chuckle.

I clench my fists. "I chase nothing." That is totally true. I don't, and I'm not starting now.

"Got news." His smile disappears as he sits next to me on the stool, grabbing my full attention. "Tried to find Dagger, but Cruz said he took off on his bike."

"Yeah, just missed him."

"Cops are on their way down here to question Mearna and Tanner. Guess the little phone chat didn't really go over with them. I knew a phone call wouldn't be enough." He and I both. "I need them to go to the safe house out on Marquette. I don't want that shit on Ravage's door. We gotta get them there tomorrow and settled a bit."

"What about this car accident Tanner came up with?"

"I'll have Tug and Breaker bust up the front of the car once you get them settled to make the story true. Mearna doesn't have to say anything except follow along with Tanner's story." Pops reaches over and grabs a beer, twisting off the cap and tossing it to the trash. "Simple, right?" Right.

"Dagger taking them out?" I ask.

"Him and you. Tomorrow morning. Get it sorted," he orders then rises from the seat.

Fuck.

I CAN'T HELP WANTING Tanner underneath me. The way she deals with life head-on, fixing shit as she goes ... The way she thought on her feet about what to tell the cops ... How loving and protective she is toward her mother ... Hell, she even shows me soft, which surprises the hell out of me.

I enter Dagger's room where Mearna is sound asleep. I look in the bathroom, thinking that's where I will find Tanner, but no such luck.

Walking down the hallway, the sounds from the main clubhouse echo throughout. I turn the handle on my room door to find it's still locked. She's nowhere. Where in the fuck is she?

I march through the main room, not seeing her, and then walk down the stairs to the basement where single room bunks are all around along with a big kids' room. We are always prepared for lockdowns, bringing Ravage family here, protecting and keeping them safe. Lately, we've had too many of those, and I'm hoping, with whatever Buzz finds out, we won't have the threat again.

Moving through the rooms, I hear the faint sound of crying from down the hall. I follow it to where the single rooms are located. Most of the doors are wide open, but one is just cracked, the faint sound of sniffles coming from the other side.

I open the door to find Tanner sitting on the floor, her

legs pulled up to her chest and her arms wrapped around them. Her head is tucked down, and her whole body is shaking with sobs. She doesn't look up or move as I step into the room. Fuck, I'm not good at this women crying bullshit. Fuck it.

I scoop her up off the floor, her head popping up with a gasp. Her eyes are rimmed in red with tears leaking down.

"What are you ...?"

"Quiet," I tell her as I sit down on the small twin bed in the room. She rests her head on my chest, and it takes a while for the sobs to soften. Only then do I speak. "Want to tell me why you're down here crying?"

"No."

I let out a small chuckle. Dagger sure was right about her being a firecracker.

"Tanner, what's wrong?"

Now it is her turn to laugh, but it's not happy. No, this is saddened to the point of hysterics.

"What's wrong? Hmm ... Okay. Let me see, Rhys." The way she snips my name out pisses me the fuck off, but I got her talking. The sooner I figure out her problem, the sooner I can fuck her. "I killed someone. I'm on the run with my mother. My mother is hurt to the point of being doped up most of the time. I pretty much lied to the cops, pulling shit out of my ass that I have no idea how I came up with. Once she gets better, I'm pretty sure I'll never be able to return home. She has no house, and no one will tell me what happened to my apartment. We have no money. I have no job. And I don't know what in the hell I'm going to do!" By the last sentence, she has pulled away from my arms and is now sitting straight, looking at me like I'm the one losing my shit.

"Babe, it'll all work out," I tell her, which makes her cackle. Fuck, I hate that laugh.

"Sure. Just like magical fairies are going to come down, poop out rainbows, and make everything perfect and wonderful."

I chuckle at her dramatics. "Stop being a smart ass."

She rolls her eyes. "You don't get it."

"I get more than you think. You've got a lot of shit weighing on you and don't know what to do. I get it. But you need to calm your shit so it can get better."

"And how do you suppose I just forget everything that is wrong and make everything better?" she asks.

"Oh, I've got ways."

Her eyes widen as she sucks in a breath.

I lean in and brush my lips slowly against hers. "I know lots of different ways, Sprite."

Her entire body full-out shivers as I feel her heart thumping in her chest.

"Want me to make you forget?"

Her eyes search mine for a moment, a storm brewing inside of them. "Yes," she whispers.

I waste not a second before kissing her, lifting her, and carrying her straight to my room. If I'm fucking her, I'm doing it in my damn bed.

I kick the door shut, turn her, and then press her against the door before lifting her hands above her head then slamming my lips to hers. The kiss is intense and brutal as hell, but she meets me at each turn, blowing my mind. She doesn't struggle out of my grip and gives in, completely melting into me.

My free hand traces the curves over her body from breast to hip, her skin so fucking soft against my rough fingertips. Tanner shifts her feet as my hand goes under her shirt, feeling her warm skin as I painstakingly inch the shirt up. I break the kiss long enough to get the shirt over her head and off her body.

Her breasts are gloriously full and gorgeous.

Tanner continues to kiss me back, not protesting in the slightest. Good.

I unbutton her jean shorts and push them down over her beautiful hips. Then I step back abruptly, needing to see her. She moans at the loss, but doesn't move her hands from above her head, even though I am no longer holding them there.

Tanner's body is sexy as fuck. Sure, there are some bruises, but who gives a fuck? A light pink lace bra holds her breasts in place, and the matching underwear only makes me want to tear them off her body. A flower and butterfly tattoo expertly weaves up the side of her body. Fuck me.

Her chest rises and falls heavily, her eyes liquid. I'm gonna make her burn with need, burn to have me inside of her. Burn.

"On the bed," I order.

Her eyes flicker as a pink tint forms in her cheeks. She hesitates then complies and climbs on the black comforter.

Watching her move that body is the biggest fucking turn on. The way her hips sway and that tight ass ... My balls draw up tight, and it takes everything in me to will them down.

"Arms up."

Tanner stills like some light went on in her head, and her body begins to coil as her thoughts begin to kick in. I move swiftly to the bed and place my lips on hers, kissing her deeply and hard. I need her to stop thinking and just feel.

Her hands come to my head, and I immediately grab them and put them above hers. I don't let anyone touch my head. When I was younger, I couldn't control that, now I can and refuse to be touched there. Tanner is too lost in the kiss to care. I feel each of her muscles relax before I pull away.

"Keep them there," I demand.

She nods her head softly in compliance.

With my fingertips, I trace the side of her face, her neck, her collarbone, feeling her skin bump and shiver under my touch. I pull one breast out, tucking the wire under it to hold it up. Then I hold her flesh in my hand and begin to massage as Tanner's body arches. Responsive little thing. Wait until I get to her nipples. I'm pretty sure I'll have to tie her down to keep her still.

I trail my tongue on the same path my fingers just made and end up at her glorious tits. I am a tits and ass man. Fucking love that shit. The bigger and rounder, the fucking better, and Tanner has that shit in spades.

I lick all around her breast, not touching her pebbled nipple, as she groans in agony. Sucking her flesh in my mouth, I give her a small nip with my teeth, and her body jerks. She has no idea what I'm going to do to this beautiful body of hers.

When I touch just the tip of my tongue to the tip of her nipple and give it a small flutter, Tanner's body wiggles.

"Settle," I command.

"I can't when you're doing that," she pants out.

I lift from her breast and search her eyes. They are dilated and on fire, just like the rest of her hot, little body. "I control this. You got me?"

She lets out a huff of air. "Control what?"

Sprite doesn't even know she's submitting. Fuck, now that's a beautiful thing, natural, none of that fake shit that I can see a mile away just to fuck me.

"Sex. You do as I say."

Her body stills at my words. "No. Sex is a give and take," she combats.

I want to laugh, but refrain. She needs to know where I stand in this scenario.

"You're right. I'm going to give you pleasure, and you're gonna take it."

"Rhys, I ..."

I move up her body quickly and kiss her furiously. I keep going until her entire body melts into the mattress. I then pull away to find her eyes are still closed.

"Tanner?" Her eyes flutter open softly. "I control this. You do what I say. I'm making you forget," I remind her.

"Okay," she says so softly I almost don't hear.

Her hands come back down to my neck.

"Tanner, do I need to tie your hands above your head, or can you keep them there?" I ask. Hell if I know what experience she has. She may have none and not know anything.

Her eyes widen. "Tie me?" She must have thought I was joking earlier. I sure as shit was not.

"Yeah, babe. You trust me to tie you up?"

Something flashes in her irises. "I'll keep them up

here." She moves her hands back above her head and grabs on to the slats of the headboard. It's good she doesn't trust me, not yet, but she does follow directions well.

Using my mouth, tongue, and the scruff of my beard, I move down her body, my cock growing and aching in my jeans. I unlatch my jeans and kick them off, my dick instantly feeling relief from the pressure.

I'm a very controlled man, and the fact that Tanner is seriously testing it isn't something I need to be thinking about right now.

I pull my shirt off and make my way between her legs where I rip her panties off before latching on to her clit, sucking hard as she bucks. I rest my arm over her hips, holding her down to the bed as I continue sucking with small nips in the process. She sets off like a rocket, screaming, but I don't let up. Fuck that. I want her coming again before I take her.

"Rhys," she pants, and my dick squeezes. Fuck, I need inside of her.

I make quick work of setting her off again, and as she erupts, I continue moving my fingers fast as my other hand puts the condom on.

"Sprite, get ready. I wanna draw this out, but can't wait."

Sliding inside of her is the heaven I know I don't deserve. I shouldn't be the one to have this right now, but I'm fucking taking it. I've never been a noble man and don't plan on starting today.

The walls of her pussy clamp down on me, and I have to halt myself for a moment to hold my shit together. I can't be coming like a fucking teenager.

"What are you ...?" Her words stop as I thrust hard into her, feeling her so damn deep I'm pretty sure I may not ever want to fucking leave. "Please," she begs.

I lose all control. It snaps like a rubber band. My hips move quickly while I latch on to her nipple and suck on it hard as her pussy squeezes me in response. Fuck, yes. I give her no reprieve, losing myself in Tanner.

I muffle her screams with my lips as her orgasm hits and mine follows. For long moments, we stay exactly like that, my lips only moving from her so I can breathe. Her pants turn me on, and I fucking want her again.

I pull out of her and roll off to the side. "Be back." I clean up and come back to the bed.

Tanner's eyes are closed, and her breathing is even. Fuck, she fell asleep. I climb into bed, pulling the covers over both of us then tucking her into my arms. I try not to think of why I'm doing this, allowing her slow breathing to carry me off to sleep.

8

TANNER

I WAKE WITH A START AND TAKE IN MY SURROUNDINGS through my grogginess. Opening my eyes, I find Rhys lying next to me, his eyes closed and his breathing slow and deep, the ripples of his chest in tune with his intakes and exhales. He's on his back, his head pointed up to the ceiling. His side profile is strong, demanding, and pronounced. Small scars play on the side of his cheek and his neck, but between his scruff and tattoos, they are hard to see. If I wasn't this close, I wouldn't have seen them. They're faint like they have been there for many, many years.

I just let this man screw me to the point that I passed out in his bed. This is not me, and it hasn't a thing to do with his age. This is not something I would do. I don't go to bed with random men and let them have sex with me, have them tell me they are going to tie me up. The few times I tried the tying up thing, it was with a boyfriend I fully trusted. Of course, it ended flat, but at least I tried. However, Rhys knows what he is doing. He knows exactly what places to hit on a woman's body to make her scream. He is definitely experienced, way more so than any man I have ever been with.

He absolutely has more ink than anyone I've ever been with, too. There's so much ink it covers his arms, neck, and part of his chest. I have to admit, it's a huge turn on.

What in the hell am I doing? I can't be with this guy. He's scary as hell. One look from that man and I swear Superman, Batman, and Captain America would crumble to the ground and beg for forgiveness. He asked me if I trusted him, and I guess I trusted him with my body, but in reality, I don't think so.

He was sensational, though. I haven't had an orgasm, or I should say orgasms, like that ever. I didn't even know I could have them to the point where all logical reasoning is completely gone, and all that is left is what you feel. It was the most wonderful euphoria I have ever experienced. Not only that, but even after waking me up through the night, this big, strong, scary man actually took care of me afterward, holding me until my tremors subsided, and then I must have passed out because I don't remember anything after that. But it was tender and, dare I say, sweet. No, Rhys is anything but sweet. Sweet doesn't even come close.

I need to get the hell out of here, get back to my mom, and get as far away from this man as I can. I can't let the way me makes me feel cloud my better judgment. This man screams bad, and I have enough bad going on.

His chest is still rising and falling steadily, so I pull the sheet up, covering my naked and well-used body, and slip out of bed.

A strong hand grips my arm, stopping me. Crap.

"Where are you going?" Rhys asks.

I close my eyes and suck in deeply, sitting up on the bed with my back to him. "I'm going to check on my mom."

His fingers flex into my flesh, giving me a slight bite of pain. The bed behind me shifts, but his touch doesn't leave. "I'm not done with you yet."

God, that man and his sexy, deep voice. My body trembles and screams at me to do it, and I try to block it out, but it seems to get louder and louder as the seconds tick by.

Rhys's other hand comes to my leg and draws lazy circles with his thumb. With each movement, nerves flair to life, and I close my eyes, breathing out deeply.

"I have to go," I tell him with what little control I have. Too bad it comes out weak and breathy. Shit.

Rhys moves his body behind me, straddling me, his front to my back, his hands around my stomach. His lips graze the curve of my neck, up and down erotically, and my head tilts, giving him better access. His hand snakes up, grabbing one of my breasts and squeezing it. Then he pulls my earlobe into his mouth and sucks hard, and sparks of want and need dance in a kaleidoscope in my belly.

"Your body's telling me you want to stay." He rolls my nipple between his fingers, giving it a pinch, and my body jerks. "See what I mean."

I try my damnedest to clear the fog that is this man, but I can't. My center is slick and throbbing. I need him to release it, to release this coil that is so tightly wound inside of me.

He wraps his arm around my hair and pulls my head back so my chin is pointing up to the ceiling. "I'm taking those fucking lips," he growls before slamming his lips down to mine. God, I love how he just takes what he wants.

I follow his lead, fully admitting that, when I'm like this, being devoured by this man, every thought, every fear, every trouble disappears, and I feel so light. This is the feeling that I crave from him, the one that only he has been able to give me.

He breaks the kiss, and I gasp for breath, finally remembering that I needed it.

"Stay," he orders, releasing my hair as he reaches for the nightstand, grabbing a condom.

As his hard erection presses into my back, my core begs for him, pleading to be taken. I clench my hands into the sheets, surprised I'm not ripping them from my strength.

My body obeys him as his hands come to my hips, and he lifts me effortlessly.

"Put it in," he orders.

I reach down, grabbing his thick length and placing it at my entrance. He only allows the tip inside of me, and even though I wiggle, it gets me nowhere. His arms are strong and unyielding.

I groan in agony. Everything he touches is on fire.

"Legs together."

I comply, and he feels even thicker this way.

"Come down on me, baby." He releases his hands, and without any help from me, he slides all the way inside my body, shocking my already sensitive nerves. I don't move, only feel every inch of him, my hands resting on his thighs for support. "Feet to the floor and one step up."

I still for a moment. He wants me to stand with him inside of me? How does that work?

Rhys doesn't wait. He pushes me off the bed, and my feet land firmly on the floor while my hands rest on my knees, holding up my body. The back of my calves touch the bed as he remains inside of me. Then he starts moving his hips off the bed, all the while holding my hips exactly where he wants them.

The slide of him inside of me builds quickly as he picks up the pace. I want to turn around and see how in the hell he's able to hold my hips and have enough muscle to plunge in and out of me, but I don't. I can't. I'm too lost in his touch. Each slide in and out touches a part of me that sizzles and flames. I just need something more to push me over. I can't ...

A hard slap comes to my hip, and I explode, the flames becoming an inferno, filling every part of my body. I close my eyes as the wails and screams fall from my lips. There is no stopping them. There is no controlling them. I can't. All I can do is let the sensations flow through my body.

Rhys slams me down hard on his lap as his arms come around my waist, holding me to his body as he releases with a grunt. We sit exactly like this for long moments as I lay my head back on his shoulder, trying to get my breathing under control. I don't know if I'm succeeding or not.

His hands brush up and down my sides as I come back to myself, his length inside of me still semi-hard.

"Morning," he growls, and I smile.

"Morning." I lift my head and try to stand up, but he holds me to him.

"Gotta get your shit packed, babe. You and your mom are getting a visit from the police, so we gotta get you away from the club."

The cops are coming? Here?

"What?" I gasp, not liking one thing of what he's saying.

"You tell the cops the same story as before. Instead of going to the hospital after the accident, you took care of your mom."

"That's the story I already told them. Do they not believe me?" I ask, a shiver crawling up my spine.

"More than likely, no, but just stick to the story, and you'll be fine."

My nerves kick up.

"I need to go talk to my mom. I need ..." I pause. What do I need? My brain starts rapid firing. "I need to get us packed up. Where are we going?"

"We've got a house a ways from here. Dagger and I are gonna go get you settled."

I should feel relieved at this, right? Then why do I feel so tense about the whole thing?

"Okay. You gonna let me up now?"

His grip tightens. "I'll be coming with you, Tanner. We aren't done." It feels more like a warning than a promise, but I have bigger fish to fry.

God, I hope my mom is doing better today.

"Rhys, let me up," I demand.

He lets out a soft chuckle then releases me. He falls out of me as I rise, and then I quickly pick up my clothes from the floor and throw them on my body.

"Bye," I say, gripping the door.

A steel band wraps around my stomach. He was so quiet I didn't even hear him get up. As his hot chest rests against my back, I should feel utterly relaxed and satisfied, but unfortunately, I don't.

"Lips," he orders, but I'm not in the mood.

"Rhys, let me go."

He turns me in his arms, his face close to mine, as I grip his strong arms. "First, you don't leave me without a kiss. Ever. Second, remember what I said; I run this." The way he says it makes my knees weak, and I seriously don't know why.

"I have to go," I tell him softly, my pulse racing again for the second time this morning.

"I have had a taste of you, Tanner, but I'm eating until I've had my fill."

I don't respond. I can't with his tongue down my throat as he takes everything from me, his mouth hot and delicious. He pulls away, and I find my lips wanting to follow him.

"Go. Be ready in an hour." He turns me, opens the door, and with a small nudge, I'm out in the hallway.

What in the hell just happened here? I breathe out hard. I need to get to my mother.

A loud whistle comes from down the hall, and my head darts to it. Princess stands there, shaking her head back and forth, but she has a smile on her face. I don't know if she's unhappy with me or if she thinks I'm crazy. I know I'm crazy, so that one is an easy call.

I move down the hall toward her—well, toward the door where my mom is.

"What did I tell you about that one, Tanner?" She

shakes her head like she can't believe me. "Girl, you don't know what you signed up for."

I huff out a breath. Maybe she can tell me.

"Care to tell me, because at this point, I really don't know." I look to the ceiling like it will give me some divine intervention. It doesn't come.

"I told you he's hardcore. Don't be surprised if he has another woman in that bed tonight. Hell, even later today. Don't get your heart involved. I love Rhys, but he bounces to his own rules." She shakes her head in disbelief. "And you are way too innocent to be caught up in that."

"It was just one night. It's not like I'm asking him to marry me or something." I'm not. No. But the thought of another woman in his bed does something to my gut, making it swirl to the point that I want to throw the hell up.

"We'll see," she says, moving away from my mother's door.

I open it to find my mother is sitting up. She's awake, but drowsy.

"Where have you been?" she asks, her words a little slow.

"I was just hanging out." Like I want to tell my mother where I spent the night. *Oh, hey, Mom, I had a one-night stand with my father's friend.* That's not something she needs to know.

When I sit on the bed next to my mom and take her hand, she doesn't flinch as badly as before. I guess that is progress. Right? She looks better today, more alert. More like my mom.

I can't lie to her, but I'm just not ready to talk to her about Rhys.

"We need to get a few things packed up. The cops from home are coming here to talk to us. The club has a place they are going to take us to so we can get questioned."

Her eyes widen. "I thought all that was done. I called them and went along with your story."

"They have more questions."

"Dammit, I bet anything it's his buddy Griff who's coming. That man..." She closes her eyes. "He'll be tough, and we need to keep our stories together."

"Why don't we just tell the truth? He was beating up on you, and I saved you."

"Because you and I both know that it's too late for that, and what the guys did ..." She trails off, shaking her head.

I don't want to think about her house blown up, either, so I change the subject. "How are you feeling, Mom?"

"Sore, but I need to wean off the pain killers, especially if the cops are coming. I need to be lucid and in control. I need to talk to Cam—Dagger to figure things out." It's nice that she has her head at least partially back.

"I'm gonna get our stuff together." I stand and do just that as my mother closes her eyes and drifts off.

———

ONE KNOCK COMES to the door, the only warning I have before it opens wide, and Dagger walks through, strong and imposing. Even if I am his blood, he still makes me nervous.

"Cameron," my mother says from the bed, opening her eyes.

"Dagger," he corrects. "You guys ready?"

"We need to talk," my mother says. Dagger crosses his arms over his chest and nods for her to continue. "If it's Griff coming, he's not going to stop until he finds out exactly what happened. He's James's partner and best friend."

"You know I'll do anything to protect you and Tanner."

"I know," she answers so honestly her eyes shine with small, unshed tears.

"Exactly. You go with the story, and everything else will fall into place." The gruffness is still there in his voice, but there is an underlying concern there that I'm in awe of seeing. "Come on. I'm going to help you to the car, and we're gonna lead on our bikes."

Just then, Rhys comes in, and the room instantly becomes smaller just from his presence. He steers right to me, not even glancing at anyone else. As his arm comes around me, and he kisses me deeply, my hands move up his arm and hold on for dear life. Any protests are sucked out of me along with the air in my lungs. He pulls away from me, and I gasp, trying to suck oxygen into my deprived lungs.

"What in the hell?" my mother says, and I close my eyes. Well, guess the cat is out of the proverbial bag.

I glare at Rhys who only smirks at me in that sexy way that makes my insides quiver.

"Nothing, Mom. Let's get us where we need to be."

"You will talk, young lady," my mother scolds, and I catch the faint smile and squint of Dagger's eyes. Glad he finds this amusing, but the thing is, I will tell her. I tell her everything. Too bad she didn't talk to me about James. We could have avoided all of this. I tap down those feelings, needing to get my shit together.

"Breaker, Tug!" Dagger yells to the open door, making me jump from the demanding sound. The two men enter the room. "Can you grab their bags?" They lift their chin then grab our very few bags. "Tanner, follow behind the bikes. Tug and Breaker will be behind you. Got me?" His brow rises as he waits for my response.

"Fine," I say, moving away from Rhys. I don't get far, as he again wraps that steel arm around me.

His hot breath comes to my ear. "Wait till I get you there. We have our own wing of the house." Oh, God. "I'm gonna make you scream."

I should deny it. I should tell him to jump off a bridge, but my body is betraying me. My body craves this man like it's my last meal. How in the hell did that happen after a single night with him?

WHEN WE PULL up to the house, it looks more like a big warehouse turned into a house. It's large like a building, but it has dormers and such over windows that make it look like a house. It's like a combo deal, and it looks nice, well kept.

"This is where we are staying?" I ask Mom.

"I guess so. It'll only be for a little bit. Once I get on my feet, we'll figure out what we're gonna do next." I should be reassured by those words, but with the cops coming, I can't help feeling anxious.

"Hopefully, everything with the cops will go well." I believe I'm trying to reassure my mother, but in reality, I'm trying to reassure myself. It's amazing how, one day, your life is relaxing and carefree, and then, the next, BAM! Everything is turned upside down, and you don't know whether you're coming or going.

I've been lucky. My mother has let go of the issue of Rhys and me for the time being. I know it's only a matter of time, but I'm thankful for the reprieve. There really isn't much I can say to her, anyways. We had sex, and that's about the extent of it.

RHYS OPENS a door down the hallway from the living room that is a huge open space with enough chairs for an army and a huge television set. It's definitely more than my mother and I need. Inside the door is a queen-sized bed with light blue covers with cream colored walls. It's not small, but not extravagant. It's actually pretty cozy.

A loud smash comes from behind me, and I jump. I'm swept up in a bridal hold, and I yelp loudly. Then I'm tossed to the bed where I bounce twice.

"What the hell?"

Rhys's hard body comes down on mine, his weight pushing me into the mattress. I don't have time to enjoy the feeling before his mouth comes down to mine as he commands my lips to do exactly what he wants. My lips are more than happy to follow his lead.

I move my hands to his head, and he instantly grabs them and secures them above mine in a tight grip. I don't know why, but I enjoy the pressure he puts on them. I like that I can forget, and he makes everything good. It's also strange that he won't let me touch him there, but just from looking at his scars, I can see he's lived a rough life. He may never tell me the reason why, but I've never asked either so that's on me.

He breaks the kiss. "I need to be inside you." He rises from the bed, pulling my jean shorts and underwear from my body, my flip-flops long gone.

I prop up on my elbows and stare at the man above me as he unbuttons and unzips his pants just enough to pull his length out and sheath it with a condom, and my core clenches. It is so freaking hot that he wants to be inside of me so damn badly he doesn't bother removing his pants. I have never felt so wanted in my life.

When his strong body again presses me down and into the bed, I raise my arms above my head just as his length plows inside of me. I scream, but quickly turn my head to press my mouth into my arm, stifling the sound. God, I hope my mother didn't hear that.

Rhys chuckles. "Give it up." He pulls my arm away from my mouth, putting it above my head as he ruthlessly takes my body, stroking in and out of me at a punishing pace. "This is gonna be quick," he grunts.

His fingers move down to my aching flesh and rub quick circles in tune with his thrusts. I come apart, trying my best to hold in the noises, but some escape because the pleasure is too powerful.

With two hard thrusts so deeply I feel him bump something inside of me, Rhys stills, closing his eyes as he releases inside of me. The lines in his face are more prominent, making him look older, and the pleasure I felt twists in my stomach.

What in the hell am I doing? This man is so much older than I am, and I have never been the type of girl who has sex with a man just for fun. I can't be doing this. Crap.

His forehead comes down to mine as we catch our breath, enjoying a small bit of reprieve.

"Rhys, I need to go check on my mom," I tell him, breaking whatever this connection is. I wiggle myself to try to get away. I need to get away. I shouldn't be doing this. I can't.

His blue eyes stare down at me and he chuckles. What is he laughing at?

"Sprite, your momma already knows that I've been inside of you. You're a grown-ass woman."

I push at his chest. "Get off." Anger overtakes me. How dare he? "So because I care that I don't do things to disappoint my mother that makes me wrong?"

He glances down to where my hands rest on the shirt he didn't take off. "Disappoint?" Something happens in his eyes. The fire that was there turns into fury, and it scares the ever-loving shit out me.

"Get off," I tell him again.

He shoves off me, tearing the condom off and tossing it into a nearby garbage can. He buttons and zips his pants, anger creasing his brows.

I scurry up the bed, press my back against the head-board, and curl my knees up to my chest, feeling utterly exposed at the moment. He's so mad, and I don't know how to fix it.

"Rhys?" I call out.

"Sprite, don't worry about it. You were a good lay. I'm out." He opens the door then slams it shut behind him, the noise so loud I close my eyes and wince.

I was a good lay. My insides squeeze. It's better to realize this now than later. Princess warned me. I just chose to listen to my libido rather than common sense.

I climb from the bed, clean myself off, and put my cloths back on, finding my flip flops by the door. My heart feels heavy, and I don't like that feeling at all.

I enter the living room where my mother sits on the couch, her feet up and a blanket over her legs. Her eyes are open and much more alert.

Dagger comes from the kitchen, holding a glass of water, and sets it down on the coffee table that he moves closer to the couch.

"How ya feeling?" I ask my mother, ignoring Dagger. I'm sure I smell of sex, but the only opinion I care about is my mother's.

"Actually, I'm good. Sore, but good. I can think, which I appreciate." She gives me a faint smile as Dagger takes a seat in the recliner.

I look over to him. "You can go now. We'll be fine."

He strokes his long beard up and down then clicks his tongue in his mouth. "Not going anywhere." His eyes bore into mine. "Why'd my brother go storming out of here?" he accuses, and it's my turn to close my eyes and look away from him.

My mother places her hand on my arm. "You want to talk about it?"

"No." I shake my head. I definitely don't want to discuss it in front of Dagger of all people.

"Sweetheart, from the noises coming from your room, he didn't sound upset." Mom's hand on my arm squeezes.

I feel the heat rise through my body and up to my face as embarrassment hits me. My mother and Dagger heard us, but in that moment, all I cared about was Rhys.

"It's fine. When are the cops supposed to be here?" I deflect as Dagger shakes his head. I don't want to talk about Rhys. Maybe, if it was just my mom, I would tell her more, but the embarrassment I feel makes me want to move on to something else.

"Couple of hours. You'll be fine. I'll be in the hallway, listening. I won't show my face unless I have to. You stick to the story and the shock of James being dead, and you'll be good," he says like he's done this so many times, and it's not a big deal at all. I don't know whether to be scared as hell or impressed.

"Is there food here?" I ask him, needing a distraction. If food is in my mouth, I can't talk.

"A few things. After the cops go, we'll head back to the clubhouse," Dagger says.

My eyes grow wide as a rock falls into my stomach. "I thought we were staying here." The idea of going back to the clubhouse when Rhys is pissed at me is not sitting well.

"Nah, it's safer there until we know what these guys want." He sees my lip curl. "You're going to see Rhys, so you better get over whatever shit you to have going on."

"Way to stick up for your daughter," I grumble, leaving the room.

"Tanner." His voice is deep and authoritative. It makes me stop in my tracks. "Club life means brothers and club before everyone, including women and children."

Things start clicking in my head fast: the reason my mother left, the reason she didn't tell Dagger about me.

"That's why ... because you'd never put my mother first in your life," I say to him.

"Tanner." This comes from my mother who eyes me to silence.

"Sweetheart, I would have given your momma everything," he says, which makes my mother gasp. "But that's not your business. You need to remember that whatever happens in the club is none of your business. The only reason we are helping you right now is because we take care of our own, but none of this shit comes down on the club."

So, pretty much I'm shit on the scale of who gives a damn.

"Whatever. We'll be gone soon, anyway, and then you can go on with your life." I dart into the kitchen, needing some space.

9

RHYS

DISAPPOINTMENT. RHYS, YOU'RE NOTHING BUT A disappointment. The sentence trails through my head on repeat. Normally, it's my mother's voice saying it over and over again, but this time, it's Tanner's.

I ride my bike hard and fast down the country roads, trying to clear my fucking mind. Regardless, those words keep running through my thoughts, pulling me down a path I thought was closed forever.

My mother always told me how much I lacked. Even if she was strung out all the fucking time, she always made it a point to put in as many jabs as she could. To a kid, that shit sticks with you. It's a fucking wound that never totally heals.

I know Tanner wasn't aware she struck a chord with me, but fucking hell, she dredged up some shit that I didn't want to put on her lap.

She's right, though. Hooking up with her should have been a onetime gig. I shouldn't have kept going with it. I should have backed the fuck off right away. I definitely shouldn't have fucking slept with her in my arms. That was a huge fucking mistake.

She's way too innocent for this life. Fuck, she's way too innocent for me, even if she melts like butter under my touch. It isn't like I am going to suck her into this life and have her stay with me. Fuck that. I don't want to be tied down. Right?

I shake my head to clear the webs of Tanner out of there. It's better this way, anyway. She needs one of those assholes who are put together or whatever.

I need to erase Tanner from my mind.

10

TANNER

A HEAVY KNOCK COMES FROM THE FRONT DOOR.

Dagger grabs my arm and pulls me into the hall. "Remember, I can't protect you and your mom unless you do as I say," he tells me, the sincerity blaring in his eyes.

"I've got it. It'll be all right." I move to the door, looking through the peephole. The first man I see is Griff, whom I met at a couple of my mom and James's parties.

I turn to my mom and nod as she closes her eyes and lets out an exasperated sigh. I then turn the knob and open the door, my nerves hitting me full force as I stare into the eyes of James's partner and best friend.

"Hello."

"Evening, Tanner. We need to ask you and your mom some questions," Griff says with all the formality and power he can muster. Crap.

"Sure. Come on in." I hold the door open, and Griff and another officer I haven't met before come in.

"Mearna, sorry to have to see you under these circumstances," Griff says to my mother, moving over to the chair across from her.

"I still can't believe he's dead," Mom says. I have to say she's pretty damn good with it. Or maybe she really does feel that way. Whichever, this is good.

"Me, either. This is Officer Miller."

Mom nods at him while I take a seat on the couch at my mother's feet. Before these guys came, I pulled out my makeup and gave her a hell of a lot of cover up, just leaving enough to make the car accident a plausible story.

"You said on the phone that you and your daughter decided to go on a road trip. It just happened to be the same day that your house was burned to the ground with James's body inside."

I turn to my mother and see a lone tear fall from her eye. My mother hasn't had it easy in life, working her butt off for everything that we had, including helping James pay for that house. Shit!

"Yes."

"Why did you decide to leave that morning?"

My mother wipes the stray tear from her face and sniffles. "Tanner kept asking me about her father, and I finally gave in. I told James where we were going, and he told me to be safe." That wasn't a total lie. I had asked about my father over and over again, but not recently.

Griff's eye twitches. "James told you to be safe. Is that all?"

Crap. Griff knows James. James would have thrown a fit had my mother said she was going to see my father. He didn't like other guys even looking at my mother, let alone for her to pick up and leave.

"Yes," my mother says with the calm of a cat purring.

"Mearna, I've known James a long time. You want me to believe that he said that?" Griff asks.

My mother looks him dead in the face. "He did."

"I don't believe you." He looks at his partner, who eyes him wearily. "There is no way he'd let you out of his sight, let alone to go find Tanner's father, who is part of the Ravage Motorcycle club from what I hear. Didn't know you were a biker bitch." The sneer in his voice has me sitting up in my seat. Here comes the Griff I've met, the one who always made my skin crawl just by being in the same room as him.

"Officer Miller, go out and check the car," he orders. "Where is it?" he asks my mother.

"Garage," she responds.

"Are you sure?" Officer Miller says, and Griff gives him a stare that would breathe fire. I really don't want the other officer to leave right now. "Okay." He gets up and walks out the door.

"I know you did something," Griff starts in the minute the other officer is out the door. "There's nothing of the body left but bones, but I know for a fucking fact that James would never let you step out of the door to go to another man. You are full of shit. Tell me what you did to him." His eyes pierce my mother and me, and my stomach falls, remembering the knife in my hand and how it felt going in and out of his flesh.

"I did nothing," my mother says honestly, because she didn't.

"Bullshit. I learned that your baby daddy is part of a gang full of criminals, gangsters, murders, drug dealers, and thugs. You want me to believe that James would allow that? What happened? He put you in your place, Mearna?"

Fury builds in my stomach and slowly begins to rise. How dare he feel that everything was okay because James was putting her in her place!

"That's enough," I cut him off.

His icy glare comes to me. "Enough of what?" he spits. "The truth? Maybe I need to start looking into this club you came to."

The fury mixed with panic rises.

"Why? We have nothing to do with what happened to James," I tell him.

"You're a lying, little slut. James told me how you threw yourself at him, begging him to fuck you. Each time, he refused."

My mouth falls to the floor, and I suck in a deep breath. "I never—"

"Save it," he cuts me off. "I believe James over you any day. You're both worthless trash." He rises from the chair, his presence making me quiver.

He moves quickly in front of me, grabbing my arm and pulling me up from the couch with a yelp.

"What are you ...?" Griff's hand comes around my mouth, muffling my words, and my mother tries to get up from the couch.

"You stupid little bitch. Maybe I'll just fuck the answers out of you," he says loudly enough for my mother to hear as he presses his hard erection into my ass. Panic like no other hits. I shake my head and scream no.

"Get your fucking hands off her," Dagger's voice comes from the entryway of the living room.

I stop struggling and thank God that Dagger stayed. Dagger's arm is extended, and at the end of it, his hand holds a silver gun. Oh, hell. He's threatening a police officer.

"Who the fuck are you?" Griff stops for a beat. "Oh, you must be the baby daddy."

"Damn fucking right, and if you don't let go of my daughter, I'll put a bullet in your fucking head," Dagger replies.

My eyes move to my mom. She's not saying it with words, but telling me though her eyes that everything is going to be okay. I sure as shit hope so.

"You won't. Officer Miller out there would have your ass," he gloats.

"Oh, you mean Matthew Miller, who owes thirty-seven thousand dollars in credit card bills, not to mention a house on the verge of getting repo'ed. Oh, and he has a wife and three children to take care of. That, Officer Miller?" Dagger's eyes are cold and stony. "You don't think I have something that will make all his problems disappear?"

Griff audibly swallows. "Bullshit."

"You didn't do your research very well." Dagger shakes his head. "We don't put up with bullshit. Let. Go. Of. My. Daughter."

A pin prickle of fear slides up my spine as Griff pushes me head first into the couch, making me hit my mother's legs.

"Give me your gun, Taser, and whatever the hell else you have on you. Slide them across the floor."

Slowly, Griff does what he says, pulling out three guns, a knife, and Taser along with pepper spray.

"Now sit your ass in that chair and tell me everything about the case." Dagger pulls out his phone, and then it looks like he's sending out a text. "Tanner, go outside and stall Officer Miller. When you hear the bikes, you'll know it's time to bring him in."

I nod, not really knowing what the hell else I am supposed to do. My mother says to trust him, and I really don't have much of a choice at this point.

I rise and head out to the door. Shakily, I move up to Officer Miller, surprised that Dagger wanted me out here alone, but he must not see this guy as a threat.

"Get everything you need, Officer?"

He turns at my words from examining the car. I suck in a gasp at the look of it. When we drove to the house it was fine, but Dagger said a couple of the guys fixed it. I hadn't seen it until this moment. The front end of the car is completely smashed in, looking exactly like it ran into a tree, just as we told Griff over the phone. I try to hide my reaction quickly.

"Looks cut and dry to me. Are you all right after this big of a hit?" he asks in concern.

"I'm fine." I place my hands in my back pocket. "My mom got a little banged up, but we're good."

He goes around the car, snapping a couple of pictures and writing some things down in his notebook while I stand there and watch him.

"Shame what happened to James," he says at the front of the car.

"Yes. My mother loved him." That isn't a lie. She did until he kept hitting her.

"Understandable."

While the seconds tick into minutes, I feel the anxiety

building up quickly. Finally, the low rumble of a motor-cycle comes from the distance, and I close my eyes, feeling the comfort surround me with the sound. As the bikes pull into the driveway, Officer Miller comes to stand next to me.

My eyes are glued on Rhys: the way his muscles flex as he maneuvers the bike—heck, the way he looks on the bike. I've never pictured myself having a thing for a guy like Rhys, but it's there.

Even though when he left earlier, it freaked me out, I have never been so happy to see him. He along with several of the club members turn off the engines to their bikes.

"Your father?" Officer Miller asks.

"No," I answer.

I don't wait and practically run up to Rhys and wrap my arms around his neck tightly, sticking my head into his leather and shirt. I feel the tears threatening to fall, but I breathe deeply in and out as his arms come around me. His gloved hands come to the top of my head as he just holds me, my body deciding it's the time for tremors to begin. I don't care that he went out of here pissed only a little while ago. None of that matters. What matters right now is that I feel safe in his arms.

"Sprite, where's Dagger?" he asks into my hair.

"In the house. He told me that, when you guys showed up, I was supposed to bring Officer Miller back into the house," I tell him, not lifting my face up, sucking in his scent like I'll never get a whiff of it again, instead.

"Has he been bad to you?" Rhys asks. When I shake my head into his chest, his hand rubs up and down my hair. "Good, baby. Good."

"Rhys," Pops calls out.

I jump, almost forgetting that all of the guys are there and the hell that I'm in.

"House," he answers. "Officer Miller, come with us."

"What's going on?" the officer asks from behind me.

"In the house and we'll explain."

Shuffling happens behind me, but I don't move my head out of Rhys's shirt. I hold on to him with everything I have.

"If Dagger wouldn't have been here, he would have raped me," I confess, a tear falling from my face.

"Who?" Rhys's body goes taut as the word is barked out, making me jump.

"Griff. In the house."

He pulls away, and my arms try to tighten to keep him close, but he's definitely stronger than I am. His index finger comes to my chin as he raises it so I'm staring into his fiery depths.

"That fucker put his hands on you?" he growls.

I merely nod my head because his angry face is scary, but I also feel so safe with him. What in the hell is wrong with me?

"Let's go." He leads me into the house, and I notice all the other guys except Breaker are already inside. Breaker follows us.

Rhys wraps his arm around my shoulders, and I feel cocooned in his warmth.

Entering the living room, I stop dead. Griff is tied with duct tape to a wooden chair that was in the dining area, and Officer Miller is sitting on the couch, wide-eyed. Holy shit, what's going on?

My mother's eyes meet mine, but she doesn't seem as shocked as I do.

"What's going on?" I ask Dagger who is walking behind Griff, the anger rolling off him.

"Tanner, take your mother into her bedroom and shut the door," Dagger orders me, making my spine stiffen. I want to know what the hell is going on.

Rhys squeezes me. "Go."

I look up at him. Something in those commanding eyes makes me listen. I help my mom up and move her to her bedroom.

"Mom, what is going on?" I ask after setting her on the bed and shutting the door. "We can't let them kill them!" I screech, but it's quiet, only for my mother to hear.

"Come here." She pats the bed beside her, and I sit. "Honey, I brought your father into this mess. We have to let them deal with it. I believe fully that he will protect us no matter what."

"But, Mom, they're police officers! Don't you think it's gonna be suspicious if they don't go back?" I mean, seriously, am I the only one here who is thinking clearly? "And Dagger already said the club comes first! He's not going to put us over the club."

"Calm down. You have to trust that he will protect us."

"You want me to trust a guy I've known for days?"

"You trust Rhys? His arm around your shoulder tells me he's pretty protective of you."

I fall to the bed next to my mom and stare at the ceiling. "Things with him can't work, Mom. There are just so many things wrong with him and me."

"You don't think I know that? You don't think it killed

me to leave your father? You don't think I have my own regrets?" my mother says.

I turn to her. "You're mad you left? I thought you were happy you left?"

"I don't know anymore. Just being around that man ..." Her voice trails off.

I need to deflect her. "What do you think the guys are doing?"

"I have no idea," she responds.

11

RHYS

I PUNCH THE MOTHERFUCKER IN THE CHEST, HEARING HIM wheeze. "Don't ever lay a fucking hand on her," I growl.

"Brother, chill," Pops says, putting a hand on my shoulder.

Fuck, I could tear this piece of shit apart. He's lucky at the moment that I'm being pulled off, because if not, he would be straight out dead. The moment I saw that terrified look on Tanner's face, I couldn't hold it back. Like a magnetic pull, I had to feel her, smell her. Protect her.

Pops steps back and pulls out a piece of paper. "Says here that you are here unofficially." That shocks me, and by the look on Dagger's face, him, too. "You took a week off to come here."

"What?" this comes from Officer Miller. "We're not getting paid to be here?" The shock on his face matches that of ours.

"No," Pops responds, surprising me.

Officer Miller sits on the couch, dumbfounded. "You

told me that the station said we had to come down here and question these two. What the hell is going on?"

"What's going on is this idiot thought he could threaten and touch my daughter. He thought he'd get some stupid confession out of them or take it out on their hide," Dagger answers.

Officer Miller stills, and if I had a heart, I might have felt something for him. "Fucking hell! I need to get back. I can't miss work!"

"Shut up! I had your vacation cleared for you," Griff spits out at him.

"You wasted my fucking vacation for this shit!" Miller responds.

"As much as this little pissing contest you have going on is humorous, we've got shit to do," I cut in. "Whose car did you drive down here?"

"Mine," Miller answers. I swear, if he were a cartoon, smoke would be pouring out of his ears.

"Good," Pops says, looking at the man. He pulls out a couple bricks of cash, handing it to Miller. Miller doesn't take it.

"What's that for?" he asks, eyeing the cash, his mouth almost salivating at it.

"You, to drive back. You speak nothing of this. Take your family on a little trip with the rest of your vacation time. You say nothing of what happened here."

Miller eyes the money then Pops. "My wife knows I'm here."

"Then you convince her that you lied," Pops responds.

"Don't you dare fucking leave. They'll kill me," Griff says.

Miller looks between all the guys. He ponders for

long moments, but I see the instant he looks at the money and realizes so many of his problems would vanish because of it.

"I'm out of here. I didn't want to come in the first place," Miller says, standing up.

Pops hands him the money. "Never a word or I find you and put a bullet in your head, your wife's, and your kids'."

Miller pales. "Not a word. Ever." He gives one more look at Griff then takes the moment. "The case was pretty much closed out after the conversation with the fiancée checked out. Griff didn't want to let it go, said the Sergeant told him to investigate to make sure. I came because he said it was ordered."

"Go," Pops says, and Miller shuts the door behind him.

"Now, this problem," Pops says, turning around while Breaker follows the cop outside to make sure he disappears. "I made a call to your wife who said you are on a fishing trip."

Griff pales.

"Tell me everything, and I'll make it fast," Dagger says. "Or don't and I'll beat it out of you. Either way will work."

I crack my knuckles, placing my fist in the palm of my other hand. I want this fucker to play hardball. How dare he touch Tanner! No one touches her. Ever.

Griff spews his guts, but everything on the case is pretty much washed up. Investigators say it was from the water heater—go figure—and closed it out.

"Tug, GT, Cruz," Pops calls out, "take this guy fishing. There's an extra car in the side wing of the garage."

Griff pales further. "You're really going to kill me, aren't you?"

Dagger slams the butt of his gun down on the asshole's neck, and he passes out.

"Boys, do good," is all Pops says as the three take Griff out. "Looks like your ladies can leave whenever they want." My stomach twists. Fuck that. "Do what you gotta do." With that, he leaves, the others following him out the door. The sound of engines firing and leaving echo through the house.

"Now what?" I look at Dagger.

"We tell them that shit's getting sorted, and they need to stay." Dagger smirks as if he's reading my mind. Sure, I'll probably get shit later for it, but fuck, having some other guy touch Tanner ... I can't do that shit. I don't deserve her, but I'm not letting her go, either.

I move down the hallway, dead set on seeing my girl. I knock and open the door.

Tanner lies next to her mother, face to face. It looks like they're talking. Tanner's head pops up. Then she scrambles off the bed and heaves herself into my arms, and I catch her with ease. Fuck, I like the fact that she feels safe with me.

I inhale her scent, not even giving a shit that her arms are around my neck. If anything, I like it. Fuck me. I'm screwed.

"I didn't mean to make you mad," she says into my neck.

"I'm not. That's my own shit. We'll talk." Even though I don't want to bring that shit up, she deserves to know that it's not her. It's all me.

"Mearna, you all right?"

Concern is all over her mother's face. I know how much Tanner loves her mother. Fuck me. Do I really have to win over her mother? This is exactly why I don't do this shit.

"I'm fine." Her eyes narrow. "What are your intentions with my daughter?"

To fuck her brains out. "Taking it one step at a time."

"Tanner," she calls out, and Tanner turns to her mother. "You be careful, sweetheart." Tanner nods, and then Mearna turns to me. "What's going on out there?"

"No worries. It's under control," I tell her.

"So if everything is under control, can we head home?" Mearna asks, watching my reaction closely. I disguise my irritation at her question.

"Nah, you two need to stay for a while. We'll know more tomorrow." I pull Tanner with me. "Come on, Sprite."

"Sprite?" her mother questions.

"I don't know where he got it, Mom, but whatever." Tanner shrugs.

"It fits you." Mearna smiles. "I like it."

All right, enough of this touchy-feely shit.

"Come on." I lead Tanner through the hallway and into the living room. She looks around, finding it empty besides Dagger sitting in the chair.

As soon as we pass, I hear the creak of the chair. He's no doubt going to talk to Mearna. I kick the door shut to another bedroom, and Tanner sits on the bed.

"Shit's gonna be wacked for a while. I want you in my bed at the clubhouse."

"Dagger said we were going back after this was over,"

Tanner says, flipping her red hair out of her face. "Rhys, talk to me."

"Babe, just roll with this shit. I don't have any answers for you. All I know is I can't get your taste off my lips, and I haven't gotten my fill of you." I sit next to her and place my hand on her thigh. Her hand comes on top of mine.

"Princess says you have your own rules, and I get that." She squeezes my hand, and I have the sudden urge to kick Princess's ass. "I have rules of my own. Princess said that you have different women all the time."

"Fucking Princess," I mutter. I'm going to get Cruz to tan her fucking hide.

"Well, I'm a one man kind of woman and expect my man to be the same. If you don't want that, then you need to leave me be." She pats my hand then removes hers, the warmth gone.

Something inside of me aches. I've never been faithful to anyone, never had any type of commitment with anyone except my brothers. I'm not sure I can do this shit.

"Babe, I ..." She places her finger on my lips.

"You're going to tell me that you don't know if you can do it." I nod my head, her finger remaining in its spot. "Would you be willing to try?" She removes her finger.

"You know you deserve a fuck of a lot better," I tell her, which makes her smile softly.

"I'm only going to be here for a short time, so it's not like I'm asking you to marry me, but while I'm here"— she grabs my dick through my jeans—"this is mine."

I chuckle. She has yet to say the word dick or cock in front of me, and I think it's pretty hilarious. She's going to have to get over that quickly while she stays at the clubhouse.

"All right, Sprite. As long as you know this pussy, tits, and ass are mine to do whatever I want with, whenever I want." I push her to the bed as her beautiful smile comes across her lips.

"Where did you come up with sprite?" she asks.

"Look at you and look at me. To me, you're little with spunk."

She rolls her eyes. "Whatever." Her face turns serious. "I'm sorry I said my mother would be disappointed. I don't know what I meant, but it wasn't—"

"Babe, that's my shit, not yours. We'll talk about it later, but not today." I roll off her and grab my cell, typing out a message to Dagger. "Tonight, we stay here, away from the club. Just you and me." I tell her. For the first time in my life, I'm actually excited about this shit.

I toss the phone down and smother her with my body. I cup her face, holding it still before I bend down and brush my lips against hers. I love the intake of breath she gives me. Who gives a shit if she's younger than me and innocent? I'm going to have fun corrupting her.

I kiss her and suck her in.

12

DAGGER

I KNOCK ON THE DOORWAY AND ENTER WITHOUT WAITING for Mearna to say anything. Fuck, this woman has put me in a tailspin. It's as if she never left.

She lies on the bed, eyes closed. The slight rise and fall of her chest tells me she's asleep. I sit in the chair in the corner of the room and just watch her with my elbows on my knees as I wipe my face with my hands.

This woman was everything to me. Everything. I would have bent over backward for her. Hell, I did. She stuck with me through the prospect period. Then we went to a party one night, and she decided she was leaving. Boom! Just like that.

I tried talking to her, finding out what the fuck happened in that short amount of time, but she wouldn't have it. I was a young, dumb kid, getting his heart shattered for the first and only time. I remember that moment when she walked out the door. "*I love you, Cameron. Always remember that.*" She kissed me, and then she was gone. Poof. It's a memory that has dug itself inside me so far there is no way I'll ever climb out. She's the one woman I loved, the one woman who changed the course of my life.

After Mearna disappeared, the old me disappeared. I didn't give a shit and fucked anything with a pussy. Hell, I still do. Even my arrangement with Flash just gives her a place to sleep. Neither one of us gives a shit about the other. I know she fucks everything with a dick, and she knows about me. It's been working for years, and she's never asked for more, so I've kept her around.

Looking at Mearna, I feel so damn old. I have ten years on Mearna, but she still looks as beautiful as she did back then. Fuck.

I feel like I should grab a pad of paper and make some fucking Hallmark card greeting or something. I can't fucking help it when it comes to this woman. I've loved her all my damn life and thought I was doing her right by not going after her when I wanted to. Fuck, once I got a lock on where she went, I was going for her to bring her back, but it didn't end up the way I wanted it to.

And because I didn't go and get her, she ended up with an asshole that beat the shit out of her.

Mearna is the one woman I would give up all the random pussy for. I'd give up Flash in a heartbeat and be with Mearna whole-heartedly. Fucking hell.

Mearna's eyes flutter open, and she takes me in. "Is everything okay?"

"Everything is handled," I tell her, not moving from the chair.

"Rhys said we needed to stay in town for a while."

"Yeah. It's best." I look down to the floor. What in the fuck am I doing?

"Cam—Dagger?" I close my eyes; my real name causes an ache that only she could give me. "Please look at me." I look up as she tries to move to sit up. Her face contorts in pain, and I move quickly to her side, lifting her up and moving her to sit up in the bed. "Thank you." She pats the bed. "Sit. I think we need to talk."

Talk. Fucking hell.

"Yeah, guess we do."

Damn those eyes. They are exactly the same, but behind them is so much hurt. All I want to do is scrub every bit of it away.

"You have a daughter," she says quietly.

I give a soft chuckle. "Yeah, I guess I do." I run my fingers over my beard. "Why didn't you tell me, Mear?"

She looks up to the ceiling like it will give her answers or some shit. "I wanted to. God, I wanted to." Her eyes come back to mine. "So many times, I picked up the phone and dialed then hung up." Her soft laugh reminds me of better times. Still love that sound. "I wanted to. I wanted to just come back and be with you."

"Then why didn't you?"

Her eyes drop to her hands that are laced in front of her. "I saw what this life consisted of. Women were everywhere, wearing nothing but scraps of fabric and hanging on to your every word like it was gold. I didn't belong here."

"I never once cheated on you, Mearna. You can't throw that shit in my face," I growl, feeling the anger begin to burn.

"I actually trust that." She bows her head. "I wasn't pretty like them. I didn't have the huge boobs or hair out to here." Her arms come out to her sides of her head, demonstrating. "I didn't speak the language that you were beginning to take on. I was an outsider. That is why I left."

"Mear, that's fucking bullshit, and you damn well know it. You left because you were scared."

"I ..." I hold up my hand, not wanting to hear the words she's going to say.

"You know you were the only woman for me. None of those bitches meant shit. I didn't fuck a single one of them, and I had a shit load of opportunities to, Mear—don't get me wrong. But I fucking kept my dick in my pants and came home to you every night."

"I know," she whispers.

"Then why'd you leave?"

She rests her head back on the headboard. "I didn't think we had a future. You were so enthralled with the club and going on runs or whatever. I felt like I didn't matter, that you didn't love me enough to pick me over the club."

And the truth finally comes out.

"Was that shit so hard to say?"

Her head pops up, and she gives me an icy stare. Fuck, I missed that shit, too.

"It's true—the club comes first—but that doesn't mean that I wouldn't protect you and keep you safe until my dying breath," I tell her in all sincerity.

A tear falls from her right eye and travels down her cheek, falling to the sheets. "It would have never worked. I was so young."

"You were young, but that's no reason to assume it wouldn't work," I fire back.

"I saw one of the ol' ladies get slapped across the face," she says quietly. "I didn't want to end up like that."

"I don't know what that situation was, but I never gave you the impression that I'd hit you, Mear. That shit belongs to the asshole that's dead right now." Her body shakes as more tears fall. "So why not tell me about the baby?"

"All you would have said to me was 'Mearna, come back,' and I would have. I was so lost without you. I wanted you so badly. I was terrified about having a baby on my own. As much as I wanted to come back to you, I knew, after I found out I was pregnant, there was no way. I couldn't expose a baby to this." She moves her hand through the air. "I cried all the time. Sometimes I didn't stop for days, just aching to be with you."

Aw, fuck it. I move to the other side of the bed, kick off my boots, and climb in. I pull Mearna into my arms and hold her as the sobs rake over her.

"You're right. I would have come and gotten you and brought you back. I would have taken care of you and Tanner."

"But a baby in the club?" Mearna says through her tears.

"Princess grew up just fine. She's been around the guys since she was born. Have you seen Casey yet?" She shakes her head. Princess is a badass bitch, and I'm proud of the way she turned out, smartass mouth and all. "That's Bam's kid and GT's ol' lady. She's in college, doing well."

"Ma did a great job with Princess," she says through a hiccup.

"You would have done a great job here, too, with me."

Fuck, I sound like a fucking pussy. Someone needs to strip my fucking man card. "It's in the past now. Tell me about Tanner."

The overwhelming sobs slow as she sniffles into my shirt. "She was born at midnight, not a minute before or after. Even the doctors and nurses said they hadn't had a baby at straight up midnight in a long time." She sighs. "She came out screaming bloody murder, and I knew she was my girl. Looks-wise, she was perfect, but she did have a small defect." Mearna's head shifts up a bit, and my stomach drops at the word defect. "She was born with a cleft palate. Inside your mouth, you have a roof as they call it. Well, she was born without it. So there was a hole from her mouth to her nose. No one could see it from the outside, but inside, there was no denying it. Feeding her was difficult because everything that went in her mouth came out of her nose."

Holy shit!

"And you dealt with all that by yourself?"

"For the most part. Tanner had to go under surgery to repair it. Two, actually. Each time, they had to put stilts on her arms at the elbow to make sure she didn't put her hands in her mouth and mess up the stitches in there." Mearna settles back into me. "After the second surgery, she was perfect. She was able to eat and drink without anything coming out of her nose. I took pictures, but I'm not sure if I grabbed them when we left."

I rub my hand up and down the softness of her arm. "How was she as a kid?"

"Trouble." She chuckles. "She was into *everything*. We had a small apartment, and I did my best to baby proof it, but she always found a way to get past it. Even locks. I have no idea how she figured them out, but she did and opened them with ease."

"Sounds like she has some of me in her."

"More than you think. Growing up, she had friends, but only certain ones. She liked being alone. She wasn't a social butterfly and still isn't. All through school, she got decent grades and ended up learning to do hair after high school. She works at a shop in town and says she loves it." Pride swarms within Mear's words, and I can't help feeling it, too.

"So she's happy?"

"She never liked James."

"Smart girl."

Mearna chuckles. "Yes." She stops laughing and almost stills. "The first time he hit me, it was bad, but I hid most of it from Tanner. Then it happened a few more times, and I stayed because he scared the ever-loving shit out me. The time that Tanner saw it, she was livid at me, but not as mad as I was at myself for putting up with it."

"Go on," I urge.

"Tanner told me that, if it ever happened again, she would get me out, and she did. That kid is the light in my life."

"I can see that."

"Sometimes, I worry that she's so put together because she's afraid I'll be disappointed in her or something. Truth is, I just want her happy. I don't care how it comes, just happy."

"Even with Rhys?" I ask. He's my brother and I love him as such, but if he hurts my baby girl, hell will rain.

Mearna lets out a deep sigh. "If that is who makes her

happy, then so be it. I will stand by her no matter what she chooses."

"What about you?" I feel like a fucking idiot as soon as the words leave my mouth, but fuck it. I've always been balls to the wall.

"Me what?"

"What makes you happy?"

Mearna rises off me so she is now sitting next to me. "Too much time has passed. We are different people now."

"True, babe."

"I'm getting old, Dagger. I'm done with the games and the broken promises. Whoever is going to make me happy is going to be straight forward and get to the point quickly. I'm not into all that courting or dating crap. It's been too long." Her arms wrap over her body protectively. "And I don't look the way I used to anymore." So that's what this is really about.

"I'm ditching Flash, and you're in my bed from now on." She gasps. "I've seen your body when the doc checked you out, and you're perfect to me. Is that straight enough for you."

She stares at me like a doe-eyed deer, and it takes everything in me not to burst out laughing at the sight.

"Why would you want me now?"

Stupid woman.

"Look, I don't play games. I'm too old for that shit, too. That being said, even after all these years, I want you in my bed, with me."

"I ..." I don't want to hear what she has to say, so I press my lips to hers, shutting her up and taking her, branding her as mine.

13

RHYS

TANNER LIES WITH HER ARMS ABOVE HER HEAD, SPREAD eagle on the bed, showing me that pretty pink pussy of hers. Fucking hell, she's hot. Her pussy lips glisten with moisture, and I want nothing more than to lick and taste her until she screams.

I slowly move up her body, using the tips of my fingers to trace up her legs. Her skin prickles as my fingers go up, and her body shivers beautifully. I continue with my fingers up her thighs to the V between her legs, but not touching the target. Instead, I move around it, up her stomach, around her belly button, and to the bottom of her breasts.

"Rhys," she gasps, making me smile.

I haven't even begun my torture of her body yet, and she's already aching for me. When I circle her nipples with my fingertips, they pull together tightly, almost turning purple. I can't believe how responsive she is to me, like she was made specifically for me. Fucking shit.

I shake that thought out of my head. Not the time for it.

Her back arches, putting those beautiful tits right in my face. I suck a nipple in, feeling it elongate on the roof of my mouth, while my hand plays with her other nipple. The noises she makes are such a fucking turn on.

I will my dick to calm the fuck down, but he has a hell of a hard time when it comes to Tanner. It's been a long time since a woman let me play like this. They never wanted to, only there for the quick fuck. Not with Tanner. Every inch of her, I want to saver and caress until I'm the only person or thing she thinks about. I want to inflame her body to the point of combustion, only leaving embers burning in its wake.

It's been a long time since I tied a woman up, but fuck me, it's something I'm craving to do with this woman right here—tie her up and never let her go.

"Let me touch you," she says breathily.

"Hands stay up there."

She groans in frustration yet listens and complies.

I take my time, giving the same treatment to the other breast and even underneath each of them. Using my tongue, I make a trail down her stomach, over to her side, up around her tit, and the same on the other side. Tanner's skin prickles and bumps with each lick. The taste of her skin is heaven—salty yet all woman.

Moving down to the small patch of red curls at her pussy, I rub my stubbly beard all over it, back and forth, just needing to mark her. I inhale deeply, smelling Tanner's arousal, and I need my sin. I need it now.

From asshole to clit, I make a huge swipe up with my tongue, and Tanner bursts on my tongue. The taste is so fucking sexy I close my eyes briefly, just to catalogue it in my head so I never forget.

I pull her to me, lifting her ass with my hands and eat her in long strokes, short fast ones, combining my fingers inside of her warm, soft pussy. She moans, mewls, and begs, but I don't relent. She tries to move her hips from side to side, but I hold her still, driving her to the brink.

Her clit gets hard as stone under my touch, and I pull back just a bit, making more languid strokes and pulling my fingers from her warmth.

"Don't stop!" she yells out, barely able to lift her head from the bed.

"Sprite, what did I tell you before? I run things. You'll get what I give you, what pleasure I give you."

"Please," she begs. I love the fucking sound of that shit.

"Hold on for me." I go back to the sin that is between her thighs and devour her, memorizing every fold and curve her pussy has.

I squeeze her ass cheeks, stopping her movement. Then I pull her clit in my mouth and suck hard. She lets out a scream, but she hasn't tipped over quite yet.

I pull away, lift her legs from the bed, and press them to my chest, her feet dangling above my shoulders. I put a condom on quickly and drive home into Tanner, who comes instantly, her legs on either side of my head coming together and trapping me.

In and out, I thrust my dick to encompass every inch of her. I want to be so deep she feels me for days so she knows I'm the one who she fucked. I'm the one who gave her the pleasure. Me.

My spine prickles, and my balls draw up. I'm going to

come, and there is no stopping it. I pound into her, rubbing her clit hard with my fingers, and just as she sets off again, I release. It hits so fucking hard I would be surprised if the top of my dick is still intact.

"Holy shit," she says, sucking in breath. I think this is the first time I've ever heard her curse, and I can't stop the chuckle. "What?"

"Just funny, Sprite. Hearing you cuss."

"Whatever," she says.

I lie down on her, her head resting on top of mine. I can feel her facial muscles pulling, no doubt into a smile. Damn, I am so fucked.

I RUB my hand back and forth on Tanner's arm. She's been sleeping for quite a while, but I need her to wake. I just got a text from Pops that we needed to get our asses back to the clubhouse now. Fuck if I know what's going on, but our alone time just got pulled short.

"Hey," she whispers groggily.

"Hey. Need you to get your stuff. We've gotta head back to the clubhouse."

Her head pops up. "Already?"

"Yep. Get dressed."

Tanner moans, but hurriedly pulls on her clothes and stuffs the rest of her things in a bag. "Ready."

"Let's go get Dagger and your mom."

I WANTED Tanner on the back of my fucking bike, but that

isn't an option when Mearna can't get on the back of Dagger's. Tanner insisted that she drive her mother, so I had to let her drive that piece of shit that we damaged. It's not the most ideal thing, but when I called Pops, he told us to get our asses back now, by any means, and this is our means. I don't like it, but it's all we've got. Dagger's leading, followed by Tanner and her mom, and then me. It's the best we can do.

One good thing, though, is the car isn't leaking shit all over the place, so it could be worse.

Pulling into the compound, Derek, the new prospect, is at the gate and waves us in. Tanner's car stalls just as we get inside the gate, and I have to swerve to miss hitting it. Fucking hell. I should be pissed, but I'm not. It's not her fault, and it's by some miracle that we even made it here.

We park and help the woman into the clubhouse. Dagger carries Mearna. Something weird is going on with that shit, but I don't have time for it right now.

Entering the main room, Pops greets us at the door. "You have two problems. One ..." He points over to the bar where that bitch Sandra is looking at me all wide-eyed and rising from the stool of the bar. "And two, we're discussing in church in ten minutes." I pull Tanner close to me, and Pops raises his brow. "Get this shit handled," he says before walking off.

"Who's that?" Tanner asks, looking up at me.

"Trouble," I grumble. "Why don't you go with Dagger and get your mom settled?" I move my arm away as she nods skeptically. Hell, I don't blame her a bit.

"Rhys, baby, where have you been? I've been trying to call you." Sandra steps into my space and locks her lips with mine.

I push her hard, and she lands on her ass in front of me. "What the fuck gives you the right to kiss me, you bitch?" Anger blazes in me. I see nothing but red. No one fucking touches me, let alone kisses me, without my consent.

"I just wanted to come and see you." She tries to stand in her slutty high heels.

"Big fucking mistake." I turn to Tanner, whose mouth is gaping. "Sprite, go to your room with your mother." She doesn't move. "Sprite!" I yell. She jumps, looking at me like I have lost my damn mind, and I pretty much have when it comes to the bitch in front of me.

Tanner says nothing, but she does walk away.

"Cruz, GT," I call out, and the guys come over. "Need somewhere to lock this bitch up until I can deal with her." Fucking bitch is a liar, and I should have dealt with her ass a long fucking time ago.

"Panic room," GT calls out. It's not really called that, but it scares the shit out of people who hear it. It's a room we can lock from the outside with no windows, so we know the bitch can't get out.

After locking her up and hearing her plead, we move to church.

"Know what this shit's about?" I ask Cruz.

"Fuck no. Pops just called everyone in." He tosses his phone on the pool table with mine.

"Girls are fine," Dagger says, entering the room. I have no doubt that Tanner is not fine. Then again, she has to know both sides of me, so I don't regret shit. That bitch Sandra has more than a little shove coming to her. I'm half tempted to put Princess in there with her for a half hour.

I lift my chin and take my seat at the large, rectangular table that has been in this room for generations. Everyone is here, including Tug, Buzz, and Breaker, the newest members of the Ravage MC.

Bang. The gavel slams, all eyes focusing up on Pops.

"What we did for Blaze is coming back to bite us in the ass," Pops says.

We all knew this day was coming. Blaze had these two assholes, father and son, who used to rape her repeatedly. She got away and disappeared here to Sumner, but they found her and tried to take her. That didn't happen. There was a huge fire fight, and we took those assholes out, instead. The problem is, those two fuckers ran with one of our major distributers that we do runs for. With them gone, I have no doubt they are losing money.

Tug's eyes could burn wood. Blaze is his ol' lady, and he would do anything to protect her. "Yeah," he says, staring right at Pops.

"Calm your shit," Pops demands, but Tug doesn't move an inch. "The assholes actually thanked us." My eyes shoot to Pops. What the fuck? "Yep, said that Santos and Frank were two assholes that they were ready to get rid of."

"Then what's the problem?" this comes from Becs, VP of Ravage.

"The guys who took over want to be compensated for how much cash they've lost."

I close my eyes. Fucking hell.

"And how much?" Dagger asks.

"Well, that's the kicker. We either pay them two hundred thousand dollars, or some of us go work for him for a week."

What in the Sam hell is going on here?

"You mean they want us to go up there so they can beat the hell out of us?" I ask.

"Pretty much," Pops says.

"No fucking way any of us are going up there," Dagger says, stroking his beard. "They'll have bullets in our heads before it's time for us to leave."

I shake my head. "No fucking way," I agree.

"All right, you want to tell me how we're going to come up with that much cash?" Pops asks. "And what's to say that, if we give them the money, they won't ask for more in the coming years?"

True. Pops is right. There is nothing stopping them from coming back over and over with this shit hanging over our heads.

"Why don't we just go to the source? Go to Ralphie. Tell him how they are fucking his shit up and work with him. Let him handle these assholes," Cruz throws in.

That shit could actually work.

"We need to find out if, their numbers got fucked up, when we took out Santos and Frank, or did they keep it business as usual?" I tell them, looking at Buzz.

"I'm almost through the last of the codes for the computer." He's been working relentlessly to break codes to get access into a computer that we believe will tell us who in the hell has been fucking with us this entire time.

"Take a break and get this shit together. I'll call Ralphie and set up a meeting. We'll all go, but it has to be soon," Pops says as he stands. "All in agreement?"

All hands rise as the gavel gets slammed down. Buzz is the first to break off as others follow.

"What's the verdict with Ralphie?" I ask GT, Tug, Dagger, Becs, and Pops, the only ones left in the room.

"Toss up. He's a bastard, so no matter what, he's not going to make it easy. As soon as Buzz has information, I'm calling," Pops answers dismissing us.

I rub my face with my hand. Fucking hell. Walking out of church, I head to the panic room. I need to take care of Sandra and shut her up once and for all, so I can get back to Tanner.

14

TANNER

I LIE NEXT TO MY MOM ON THE BED, REPLAYING WHAT I JUST witnessed in my head over and over again. If Rhys didn't think twice to put his hands on that woman, would he do that to me? After what happened with my mother, I can't deal with a guy like that. While I may feel safe and protected in his arms, the fact that those hands could hurt me at any time is like a knife to the gut. He has scared me from the moment I met him, with the tattoos lining his body and the stare that could kill something by just a single look. It's definitely not something I want in my life.

What life? Dagger and Rhys say we have to stay here, but shit. How much longer? Mom seems to be getting better, so we need to just cut our ties and leave, get away from this place. Listen to me. I sound just like my mother. Running. Since when did I turn into that woman? I'm not. I've always faced things head on and figured out ways to make things work.

I'm sure Rhys has an explanation. Right?

A slight tap comes to the door as it opens. "Hey, can I come in?" Princess asks, carrying a little boy.

"Sure." I sit up as my mother stirs.

"Who's this?" my mother asks.

"This is Cooper. Mine and Cruz's little guy." Princess's face lights up like a football stadium when talking about the little boy. He's unbelievably cute and definitely resembles Cruz.

"Hi, there," I say, standing from the bed.

"Hi. I Cooper," he says, wiggling down from his mother.

"I'm Tanner, and this is my mom, Mearna," I tell him, and my mom smiles.

"Mearna ..." He puts his finger on his chin like he's pondering something. "Like *Brave!*" he yells and looks at Princess.

"Merida is *Brave*, but close." I have absolutely no idea what in the world they are talking about. As Princess looks up at me, she smiles. "It's a Disney movie. He's watched it about a million times."

"Okay." I haven't seen one of those since I was kid. I couldn't even tell you the last one.

"I go pay?" Cooper says, looking up at his mom.

"Yep. Daddy's in church. Stay away from the doors," she orders. Cooper doesn't waste another second, darting off down the hallway. "He's a handful, but I wouldn't have it any other way."

"Cute kid."

She enters the room and comes to the bed. "So, how are ya feeling?" she asks my mother.

"Pretty good. As long as I don't move certain ways, I'm good."

"So, pretty much when you're still?" Princess chuckles.

"Not exactly, but something like that."

"It'll take a while to heal." Princess looks at me. "And you?"

"I'm good." I want to talk to her, but I really don't want to do it with my mother sitting right here.

"I have something that I want you to see. Will you come with me?" Princess asks, and elation fills me. Is she a mind reader or something?

"Yep, I'll be right back, Mom." I kiss my mother's cheek then follow Princess out of the room and down the hall. She opens a door, and we step inside.

"This is mine and Cruz's."

I nod as she shuts the door. The bed is perfectly made, something that doesn't happen in Dagger's room unless I do it, but my mother is usually lying on it. I can't complain. At least all the sheets and blankets are clean.

"Have a seat."

I take a seat on the bed, one leg bent at the knee and the other leg hanging off the bed.

Princess seems so happy in her own skin. She just exudes confidence, and I admire that.

"What's on your mind? And don't tell me nothing, because I know something's there." She sits, a mirror image to me with her hands on her legs, looking at me expectantly.

"Rhys scares me."

She laughs, full-out, no-holds-barred laughs. "Girl, he scares everyone."

"No, I know like that, but he scares me." I suck in a

breath. "Having sex with him is like no other. He does things to me that I've never experienced."

"So he fucks you right. Good for him. What's the problem?"

I sigh. "The problem is I can't distinguish between my heart and just sex. I'm not the type of girl who does that. And then ..." I trail off.

"Then what?" she presses.

"I saw him push a woman on her ass in the main room. Is he violent with women?" I twist my fingers, not wanting the answer, but needing it.

"You're talking about Sandra." She shakes her head. "I wanted to go out and beat her fucking ass myself, but Cruz wouldn't let me." I stare at her with wide eyes. "That bitch fucked this whole club, and the only reason no one touched her out there is because she's Rhys's shit to clean up. He brought that bitch into Ravage, and he needs to get her out."

"Get her out?" I ask. God, I sound so pathetic.

"Sweetheart, I know you're new to this shit, but you need to be a fast learner, especially if you want to be on Rhys's arm, and from the look on your face, you do. That's a whole other issue for another time. This right here—Sandra—she fucked with the club; therefore, she is dealt with. Most of the time, that means she will disappear and never be heard from again." Princess quirks her brow, and I read between the lines. Holy shit, they are going to kill her? "Now, to be in this club, that shit needs to roll off you."

"But ..." Princess holds her hand up, and I stop.

"It's something that is learned over time. The best

thing you can do is forget it. It doesn't exist. You are no part of it."

My mind whirls with everything she just said. They kill people. Is that what they did to Griff and Officer Miller? Did they just make them disappear?

A hand comes to my arm, and I look to Princess.

"I get that you're freaked out. This isn't the life you were a part of before. This is our life. This is how we settle scores. If someone comes after us or ours, then we take them out."

Princess proceeds to tell me several stories. One is of her fighting for her son Cooper when he was kidnapped by his biological mom, which shocked me. It ended with several dead. One is where the old president of the club was gunned down and the retaliation that took place. Then there were the things that happened to Blaze that are beyond terrible. However, the thing that sticks out to me most is that each of those men had each other's backs. They may put the club first, but they never hesitated to take care of the women and families.

"I don't know what to say." I sit there, speechless, playing all the new information in my head over and over again.

"You are part of this life now. Dagger is your father, and we have enemies. Don't be surprised if you have protection of some sort."

"What?" I breathe.

"There seems to always be shit going down or coming up. Protection happens, and with you not knowing this world, I'm sure Dagger will be extra cautious with you and your mother." She raises her brows. "What's going on there?"

I shrug. "No clue. I've got enough going on." I'm not sure how I feel with Dagger getting close to my mom again. I don't know where that would leave any of us in the long run. "We'll be leaving as soon as we get the okay and Mom is better."

"You're really going to go home?"

"Of course, why wouldn't we?"

She eyes me, and I feel a bit freaked by the inspection. "Because you're sitting ducks up there."

"We'll have to go back for the funeral." That reminds me. "I don't even know when that is, but surely my mother would need to go." I make a mental note to do a Google search.

"You need to talk to Dagger about whatever you choose to do." She eyes me skeptically.

"What?"

"Why do you want to leave? Guy at home or something?"

My mouth gapes. "No. I wouldn't be with Rhys if I did." Princess laughs. "Seriously. I'm a hair stylist, and I need to get back to work for cash. I'm not hurting, but being off too long isn't going to do me any good."

"Really?"

I nod.

"I could use you at the club," she says.

"What club?"

"X. It's a strip club. Gotta have someone to keep the girls looking good. The better they look, the more money we make."

"You own a strip club?"

"The club does, but it's my baby. I built it from the

ground up. Blaze helps me run the place. I'll take you there sometime soon so you can see for yourself."

I don't know whether to be flattered or run the other way. "Thanks?" It comes out as more of a question than a comment.

"You sure are innocent. No wonder Rhys is drawn to you."

"I told him what you said about him having someone else in his bed. I told him that I don't do that. It's either me or not."

"Shit," Princess grunts. "Oh, well. Good for you. I hope for your sake that it works out that way."

I'm a bit confounded, but power on. "You think he can do it?"

She shrugs. "No idea."

Bang, bang, bang comes to the outside of the door, and my eyes dart to it.

"Princess, open the fuck up. I need Tanner."

Rhys. I don't know whether to be nervous or excited. He has me all twisted in knots.

"Come in," Princess yells, and the door flies open, crashing into the wall. "Damn, be careful. Cruz hates to have to replace doors."

"You're lucky all I'm doing is blowing your door off," he growls, and with the shiver going down my back, I don't know if I'm excited or afraid.

"I know. I know. Tanner already told me. At least it's out of the bag, and you both know what you're getting yourself into," Princess says as he stalks into the room.

He points at Princess. "I'll have Cruz deal with you." Those eyes meet mine as he pulls me from the bed by my hand. "Come on," is all he says as I wave bye to Princess, and she stifles a giggle.

He pulls me down the hallway.

"Rhys, where are you taking me?"

Two seconds later, we are in his room, and he has me up against the door, his lips on mine, devouring me. I melt into him. Shit, he can kiss. What was I supposed to be thinking? Forget it.

The hardness of the door behind me makes this feel erotic and different. I've never had a man who needed me so badly he had sex with me against a door because he couldn't wait. This would make twice that he's blown my mind doing these things.

Down on all fours, he takes me hard and rough. I love every second of it. So much so, I pass out.

———

"HOLY SHIT," I whisper, walking into Studio X, the strip club that Princess runs. She insisted that I come with her tonight since the guys had club business and asked Ma and Cooper to stay with my mom. I didn't balk at the idea, because truth is, Princess is kind of scary, and I'm glad I'm on her good side.

The entire place is blood red and black. It gives off almost a classy feel, if that is possible for a strip club. Men line the floor around the stage. A woman with only a thong and a small scrap of fabric over her breasts works the huge stage while other women work the small side stages on either side of it. They line the whole back wall of the place. A huge bar with tons of people lining up to get orders is on the other. Small tables and chairs fill the space, and lights flash every which way with a spotlight on the dancer on the big stage.

"Welcome to my baby," Princess says, pulling me out of my amusement. "This is X." The smile on Princess's face is huge, showing me her pride in the place, and I can see why. Men hold up money like it's scraps of paper they found lying on the floor. Some are even throwing it at the dancer as she moves near them.

Between the whistles and the music, my ears are thumping hard.

"Come on. Let's go see if Blaze in the back." She walks toward the back of the space as I follow quickly through a heavy, velvet curtain where a guy nods at Princess and looks me up and down, assessing.

"You new here?" he asks in a deep voice, and my eyes widen.

He thinks I'm coming to strip here? No way. I would never have the guts to get out there in front of all those men and expose myself. Between my ass and tits, I'm not sure I would fit the profile.

"No," I say, making his smile falter.

"Shame. With an ass like that, I'd love to give you a ride," he says just as Princess steps in his face.

"Doug, this is Rhys's woman."

The man's entire body stiffens, and his mouth opens and shuts, but no sound comes out.

"You want me to tell him you're hitting on his woman?" His head shakes emphatically. "Then do your job and keep your fucking hands to yourself." Princess growls exactly like the guys do when they are pissed off. Guess growing up there did turn her into one of the guys.

I think for a moment about my life if I had grown up

here. Would I be like Princess? All badass and scary? Would Dagger have taught me about the club and what everything means? Would my mom and I have been happy?

I push those thoughts aside and follow Princess into the well-illuminated back, giving Doug a small, apologetic smile. Poor guy didn't need his balls in a sling.

Girls in various stages of dress flitter throughout the room in a whirlwind of commotion. Some are at lit-up makeup tables, putting their faces on and fluffing their hair, while others are putting on, taking off, and adjusting what little clothes they have on. It reminds me a lot about the club mommas I've been learning about.

The rustling sounds of the back area muffle out the boisterous music from the dance floor.

The beautiful brunette I now know as Blaze is sitting on the floor with a needle and thread, sewing one of the girls' barely-there shorts that ripped as we walk up to her. Her eyes lift briefly, the needle with a long piece of hot pick thread dangling from her lips. She clasps it, pulling it out and begins to sew the woman's shorts.

"What's going on, ladies?" she asks, her attention on her task.

"Showing Tanner around. You know she does hair?"

Blaze stops and now looks directly at me. "No shit?"

"No shit," I say back with a smile.

Blaze goes back to her sewing as she talks. "We could use you around here. Some of these women need some serious help with their color and cuts."

"Hey," one of the girls chimes in, but she is silenced at Princess's intense glare. I take it she runs a very tight ship here, and not just that, but I get the feeling the woman here really respect her.

"I'd be happy to help while I'm here, but I don't know how long that it'll be. Mom's supposed to get a call tomorrow to let us know when the funeral is, so I suppose, after we go to that, we'll just stay up in Tennessee," I say, still looking at all the motion in the room. It's actually very intriguing seeing how things work backstage. I've never had the opportunity to do this before.

Blaze looks up from the shorts at Princess, who gives a soft smirk. "You really think you're going home?" she asks, tying a knot in the thread and cutting it with scissors.

"Thanks, Blaze," the woman says as takes her shorts before scampering off quickly to the makeup table.

"Yeah, I have to go home. I have a job, and I'm sure my mother wants to go back." After I say the words, my mind races. Would my mother want to go back home? There isn't really anything keeping her there now. She doesn't have a home and only a few friends.

I make a mental note to talk to her about that when I get back to the clubhouse. The scary thing is I don't know if I want to go back. I shake my head.

"What about Rhys?" Blaze asks, tossing her thread in a basket and rising gracefully to her feet.

What about Rhys? Isn't that the million dollar question?

"What about him? We both know this is a fling. He knows I'm leaving, and I'm sure he's happy about it. I know he's not the staying type, but he did promise me it would only be me while I am here," I tell them as they usher me into a room and shut the door. It's set up with the same makeup mirror as outside with a large couch that I'm pulled to and led to sit on.

"Wait. You said you told him you didn't want him to sleep around, but you never said he told you he would try. He seriously agreed to that?" Princess asks. From her tone, she is truly surprised at that little revelation. To be honest, so am I. I just hope he means it.

"Yep. You think he can do it?" I don't want to know the answer, but at the same time, I do. I don't know much about the man, only what Princess told me. But it's him. His presence is so over the top and powerful. I'm sure he could have anyone he wanted, and those mommas are dying to get their hands on him.

As the two women give each other a look, I wish I knew them well enough to know what it means. However, I fear it's not good. It's only for a few days. Surely I can keep him sated enough that he doesn't need to go looking for anyone else.

Before he left for the day, we screwed twice. I've gotta hand it to him, though; for being older, he sure has a hell of a lot of stamina.

"I don't know, but it'll be interesting to find out," Princess says, leaning back into the couch. "See, Rhys doesn't open up much. As long as I've known him, we've never talked, and I never have learned anything about his biological family except he doesn't have any contact with them." She shrugs. "Rhys is Rhys." In other words, if he wants someone else, he'll do it without question. If he does, though, we'll be over. I'm not that kind of woman. Sure, they are out there, but he'll have to go searching for that one, instead, because I'm not her.

"Whatever. I'm sure we'll be leaving here soon enough, and I won't have to worry about any of it," I tell them, feeling a small pang of dread hit my gut, but I shake it off.

"Well, we've got shit to do. You wanna hang back here with the girls, or you wanna come out on the floor?" Princess asks.

"I think I'll see if any of them need help with their hair. It'll give me something to do." And stop all the thoughts of leaving Rhys from plaguing my thoughts.

"Sounds good. I'll be back here off and on," Blaze says, standing up. "Gotta check some numbers and I'll be right back." I have no idea what she is talking about, numbers? But whatever.

After they take off, I find the girls very welcoming as I offer to do their hair. Blaze wasn't kidding about these ladies needing colored and cut. Some of them have hair that is so beat up I'm surprised they can get a comb through it.

After a couple hours of hair, I feel light and back in my game. It's only been a couple of days, but I miss doing it. It's been a passion of mine since I was a little kid. I feel calm and more centered now.

Princess and Blaze haven't come back from wherever they went. I push open the heavy curtain blocking the back from the front. Doug smiles at me and says nothing. He must be really scared of Rhys. I can't say I blame him.

There are twice, maybe triple, the amount of people now crushing the room. By the sixth excuse me, I give up and just start barreling through the crowd, hoping to get to the bar. At least I can get a drink while I look for them. I figure my jeans, pale blue shirt, and toned down hair will tell all the guys that I'm not a dancer here. There are a few women, but men are the majority.

An arm comes around my waist, pulling me into a hard, pudgy stomach. My hands immediately fall on the one gripped around me.

"Look what we've got here." The man's alcohol-laced breath comes to the side of my face, and I want to gag.

"Let go," I tell him, wiggling out of his grasp. Unfortunately, he's strong, reminding me of James. Heat pours through me at that thought just as two more men step to the front and beside me. Oh, hell no.

Rearing back with my elbow, I give him a savage thrust into his gut at the same time I stomp hard on his foot, thanking God I wore boots. His grip loosens, and I move, but I don't get far before one of the guys snatches me and the other slaps me hard across the face. The burn from the blow radiates through my face and down my neck.

I pull my chin to my chest and slam my head back hard into the guy holding me. From the wetness on my neck, I know I at least bloodied his nose.

His arm leaves me as he starts calling me a stupid bitch and saying, "I'll get you whore." The guy who slapped me grabs my hair and pulls it hard, each strand straining to stay inside my scalp. He begins to drag me, but I refuse to let my feet move. Where in the hell is security in this place?

My hair is abruptly released, and I tumble to the ground from the force of trying to get it out of the man's grasp. My breaths come out in pants as I rush to my feet, assessing my surroundings. Rhys stands in front of me, his eyes full of unleashed fury.

My heart races. I have to admit, he's scaring the shit out of me with that look.

"You okay?" His tone is angry and fierce.

Instead of words, I nod my head just as Princess runs out of the crowd, coming to stand next to me.

Rhys turns behind him where Dagger, Cruz, GT, and the other brothers are holding the guys with their arms behind their backs as the scramble to try to get away from them.

"Princess," Rhys says, eyeing her.

"Got it." She pulls my arm. "Come on. Let's get you up to the office. Blaze, make sure everything is smooth," she calls out as we walk up a curved staircase that has a wide view of the floor below. My eyes immediately find Rhys, who is throwing punch after punch on the guys who tried to hurt me. My eyes well with unshed tears, the actions of the men racing through my head.

Princess pulls me into an immaculate office in the same black and blood red as downstairs. She leads me to a chair and has me sit. I don't move, too stunned, as she comes back and places something cold in my hand. I look down to the bright blue ice pack and remember the fire in my cheek. I place it on the side of my face with a wince.

"What the fuck happened out there?" Princess questions, sitting on the edge of a huge desk, her eyes pinned on me.

"I was coming out to find you and Blaze ..." I tell her everything in a rush, not taking a breath as I explain.

"Fuck. I'm gonna kill those fuckers," she growls.

"The guys?"

She smirks. "Fuck no. The boys are dealing with those asses. I'm talking about my security. This shit isn't

supposed to happen here, and they damn well know it."
She pulls out her phone and types something then sets it
down.

"What are they gonna do to them?" I ask. My head
and jaw hurt, but I've had worse, and I'm not about to let
it get to me.

"Teach them a lesson, ban them from the club." She
shrugs. "Who knows what else?" Just like they did with
Griff. A shiver quakes me. "It's my fault. I should have
told you to stay in the back or call me if you wanted to
come out." Princess moves to the chair behind her desk
and takes a seat.

"You couldn't have known," I tell her because there is
no way she should blame herself for the actions of a few
morons. "I'm sure it'll all work out, right?" I don't know if
I am trying to reassure her or myself at this point.

"I'll have to fuck up security again. Motherfucker."
She picks up her phone, speaks into it, and then slams it
down to the holder. "Blaze is coming."

I nod. "Why 'again'?" I can't help asking.

"When Blaze danced, she had an asshole jump up on
stage and tackle her. Tug took care of the guy, and I upped
security, or so I thought." I don't process most of what she
says. I'm stuck on the Blaze dancing part. She's beautiful,
and I bet she brought home a serious amount of cash. I don't
ask, though, even if it's on the tip of my tongue to do so.

The door burst open behind me, and I leap to my feet,
dropping the ice pack to the ground. Rhys stands at the
door, heaving with blood dripping from his hands.

I clutch my hands together and put them against my
chest, knowing his mood is anything but happy.

"Come here," he orders, the rise and fall of his wide chest and flaring nostrils freaking me out. He's so pissed right now I'm not sure I should go to him, so I hesitate. "Sprite," he says tersely.

I can't stop my feet from moving toward him, my body trembling the whole time. Not that I believe he would hurt me; it's just the first reaction. After James and then what just happened, I can't stop the fear.

His hand cups my chin, turning it so he can look at where the asshole punched me. I have no doubt it's red.

"It should mix in well with all the other fading bruises." I wanted my tone to come out teasing, but it's more flat, and Rhys hears it.

"Fucker won't touch you again." He pulls me roughly into his arms, and I wrap mine around his back, barely able to meet my fingers.

The nerves that were spiking uncontrollably begin to settle at his touch as I burrow myself into him, my face in his neck. I soak every bit of comfort I can from him and let his strength settle me.

His hand moves up to my hair, leaving fire on my skin as he threads his fingers through my tresses. I wince at the touch.

"Fucker pulled hard?" he asks, already knowing the answer.

"Yeah. I wouldn't be surprised if I left some on the floor out there." My words come out muffled into his neck, but I'm not ready to move yet. I want to stay right here in his warmth.

I ignore all the warning bells going off inside of me, telling me this is a bad idea. I shouldn't feel this way with this man. Nevertheless, I cast it all aside and soak in the moment with him.

"I'll kill that son of a bitch." Those words make me move quickly.

I look into Rhys's eyes that are filled with so much clouded anger I'm not sure I could help him at this point. "You can't kill him. You'll go to jail," I whisper, moving my hand to his face then stopping myself. He doesn't like to be touched there, I remember. I place my arm back around his waist.

Princess laughs from the other side of the room, but says nothing.

"You let me worry about those dickheads. I swear to you, they will never get near you again."

I burrow my head and inhale deeply. Rhys smells like wind, outdoors, and plain out sin. I can't get enough of it.

He pulls my head out the crook of his neck and kisses me hard. I don't resist falling into the hungry kiss and enjoying every second of it. When he pulls away, I whine. I want his comfort. I want him.

"Sprite, stay with Princess for a bit. I'll be back in a few, and you're on the back of my bike." He kisses me again, releases me, and like smoke, vanishes quickly.

"Well, fucking hell," Princess says.

I stare at the door, willing him to just come back and hold me, but he doesn't. Instead, I grab the ice pack and put it on my face.

I look up into Princess's dancing eyes. "What?" I fall down into the chair, my legs sprawled out and head resting on the cushion. My head feels so heavy.

"Sister, Rhys doesn't put women on the back of his bike. Ever." None of this means anything to me, so I stare at her. She shakes her head, coming closer to me. She stops, her eyes squinting in thought. "Remember I told you about biker hard?"

How the hell could I forget? It scared the shit out of me.

"Yeah."

"Part of biker code is only allowing women on the back that they choose. Rhys doesn't allow any woman on the back of his bike. In all the years I've known him, I've never seen him take one."

My eyes narrow. "And this is some big deal?"

Princess chuckles. "Tanner, are you ready to be Rhys's ol' lady?"

I still, my body not even taking a breath. Princess has lost her mind.

"I'm only here for a bit longer. I'm sure the funeral is in a couple of days, and we'll have to head back."

"Whatever you say, but don't say I didn't warn ya."

15

RHYS

MOTHERFUCKING PIECE OF RAT SHIT. I GRIP THE PLEADING man's hair and pull as hard as I fucking can, wanting him to feel the hurt he put on Tanner.

His screams do nothing to stop the thunderstorm inside of me. I want his flesh. I want him a quivering fucking mess. I want him dead.

I pull the fucker hard again as Dagger begins his assault on the asshole's ribs and stomach. Nothing like having the full wrath of both Dagger and me come down on you. I don't fucking care. Cruz and GT are taking care of this asshole's friends, leaving him to us.

"Don't ever fucking touch my daughter!" Dagger unleashes blow after blow, the man getting limp in my arms.

His hair begins to tear in my hands as his weight plummets to the ground. I rub the hair in between my fingers then throw it to the ground, giving him three hard kicks to the ribs.

"Enough," Pops calls from the sidelines. Fuck, didn't even hear him walk up.

I stop my foot mid-kick and set my booted foot to the black-topped ground. There's nothing like beating a guy in the parking lot.

"Get the fuckers' IDs and leave them."

"Just let me end him," Dagger says to Pops.

"You don't think he knows he fucked up? Look at him. He's got fucking dress pants and loafers on. He's learned his lesson." I hate it when he's right, but the chances of this asshole coming back are slim to none.

Dagger kicks the guy in the face, his head snapping back hard. No sounds come from him; he's out cold.

Fine. I grab his wallet, taking all the cash, which is a pretty good wad, and grab the ID. I'll have Buzz track the fucker and make sure he doesn't come close to Ravage or Tanner again.

Cruz and GT hand me the cash they pulled with the IDs.

"Why the fuck you giving that shit to him? She's my kid." Dagger's eyes narrow. He's itching for a fight. He didn't get enough of his frustrations out on these assholes and still has it pent up. I've known Dagger for-fucking-ever and know exactly what he needs.

I shove the bills and plastic in my back jeans pocket and stand tall, crossing my arms over my chest.

"Because Tanner's fucking mine," I say before I even think about what I'm saying. It wasn't what I intended to come out, but it's out there.

"Yours?" Dagger scoffs. "For how fucking long? A day, two? Fuck you," he barks back. To be straight, his words don't bother me. If anything, it's the truest he's said, but under the dark veil of night, with Dagger's blood pumping, I egg him on.

"Until I'm fucking done with her." This is an asshole-ish thing to say when, the truth is, I'm not sure I'll ever get enough of the strawberry blonde.

"You prick." Dagger comes at me full force, and I let him get a couple of punches in before I fight. He and I go head to head, the crack of flesh against bone echoing through the dark. Sure, he hits hard, and I'll have some serious bruises, but I hit him just as hard, leaving the same marks. This is good, old-fashioned fighting: no guns or implements, only our hands and fists. I fucking love it.

"Stay away from my daughter," he roars, giving me an uppercut.

I repay him with the same. "No."

"You fucking hurt her, and I'll tear you apart," he growls at me and I smile. Seeing Dagger go all dad is seriously different, but I know everything coming out of his mouth is out of his pent up frustration.

"Wouldn't expect anything less."

Our blows continue to ensue. I can see the moment when Dagger has released the anger, and I back off.

"Oh, my God!" Tanner's voice has my eyes swinging to the door. Her face is wide in shock as tears well up in her beautiful eyes. "What are you doing?"

Princess trails behind her with her hands up in the air. "She's stubborn as shit. Could have subdued her, but what's the fucking point?" she says in her defense.

Tanner rushes up and stands between Dagger and me. "Don't do this. Why are you doing this?"

Dagger has full-out calmed himself, the fire in his

eyes dying down to an ember. "Tanner, relax," he tells her.

Her eyes grow cold. "Relax? You want me to relax? My father and ..." She looks at me, the wheels turning in her head as she tries to explain our relationship.

Fuck it. I do it for her. "Man."

She shakes her head. "Whatever are beating the hell out of each other in a parking lot. What is going on?"

I walk up behind her and wrap my arms around her waist, pulling her flush with my body as Dagger steps forward, a small smirk playing on his bloody face. "It's good, Tanner. Rhys was just helping me get some shit out."

Tanner's body tightens in my arms, and I squeeze harder.

"By hurting each other?" She shakes her head.

Dagger's hand comes to Tanner's face, and she stops moving as he looks down at her. "I know you don't get it, and that's okay, but everything is fine." Dagger looks up at me, lifting his chin. "Thanks, brother, I needed that."

I just lift my chin in recognition.

"I don't understand you at all," Tanner says, putting her weight into me, and I take it.

I lean down to her ear. "Sprite, everything is fine."

Her head turns to mine and she gasps. "Oh, God, you're bleeding." She tries to scramble out of my arms, but I don't allow her to move.

"It's all good."

"But ..." she sputters. Then I can feel her back straighten. "Come inside so I can clean you up." She grabs my hand and pulls me back into the building. I allow it because she needs to have the break, and I truly need to get cleaned up before we head back to the clubhouse. If the cops stop me looking like this, I'll be pulled in for questions.

X is still pumping, the dancers on stage doing their thing. For as tiny as Tanner is, she sure makes a quick path, taking me back to the dressing room. I lift my chin at Doug the guard at the curtain who says nothing as we pass.

"Oh, my God, Rhys!" One of the brunette dancers rushes up to me, placing her hand on my arm. Tanner says nothing, but the tick in her cheek tells me all I need to know. I brush the bitch off and move to the bathroom. Tanner follows and looks under the stalls while I lock the door. She says nothing of the confrontation, but I can tell she wants to.

"Yeah, I fucked her. I've fucked most of the women here. They're easy." I have no issues with my past. Why should I? I am who I am.

"Whatever. Sit." She points to the counter, and I quirk my brow. It's cute how she thinks she's going to tell me what to do, but I appease her and sit. Fuck, this woman has me in knots.

She grabs paper towels, wetting them, and then begins to swipe the blood from my face. I watch her intently, noting each movement as she works wordlessly.

The redness on her cheek is beginning to bruise. It'll be nasty in the morning, but I've unfortunately seen her with worse.

Her brows narrow as she takes in each cut and scar on my face and neck. My tattoos hide most of the scars, but when someone is up close, they aren't hard to miss. Each one of those scars made me the man I am today and don't bother me in the least.

"Wash your hands," she orders, stepping back from me and throwing the wad of towels into the trash.

I hop off the sink and wash them. They burn, but no matter. I blot them off with the paper towel she's holding, and I can tell the gears in her head are moving so fast I swear smoke will come out of her ears at any moment.

"I get it," she says quietly.

I toss the towel away then lean my hip on the sink, giving her time to sort whatever is in her head out.

"He was pissed. Judging from the guys lying on the ground, it didn't help him, so you did." Her emerald eyes meet mine, shining. "You helped him." I shrug. "Don't do that," she orders and steps into my space. I uncross my arms and put my hands on her luscious hips. "You fought with him to let him get it out. It's strange, but I get it."

I pull her into my arms, her face resting in my neck, her arms around my waist. I'm learning fast that this is one of my favorite positions for her.

"It's good, Sprite. He needed to get it out."

"And you just let him ..." Her voice trails off with a slight tremble. I squeeze her tightly and feel the wetness from her tears hit my shirt. Fuck me.

"Sprite, it's okay."

She shakes her head, her hair rustling back and forth as I glide my hand up and down her back. Crying women is really not my thing, but with Tanner, my body just knows what to do.

I let her have her time, getting out everything that happened throughout the night. Once her body is boneless against mine and I'm holding all of her weight, I pull away and look into her red-rimmed eyes. She sniffles.

"Sprite, let's get back."

She nods.

My body needs to rest. I'm not as young as I used to be. I can take anything handed out to me, but I would be a fucking liar if I said my body didn't ache from the blows.

16

MEARNA

"ARE YOU UPSET YOU LEFT?" MA ASKS ME, MAKING everything inside me twist.

That's a loaded question if I ever heard one. Leaving Cameron was the hardest thing I ever did in my life, right next to raising Tanner alone.

"I've always wondered what my life would have been like if I'd stayed." If I had given us a chance... if I had been with him through the entire pregnancy... if ... if...if. Life is full of what ifs, but I'm choosing to move forward from here. "But I can't change any of that. It is what it is. I can't look back anymore." Lord knows, I've been doing it a lot in my dreams ever since we got here.

"No, you can't look back, but what are you going to do moving forward?" she asks.

I shrug. "I haven't got a clue," I tell her honestly.

The way that Cameron kissed me back at that house sucked me in, and I was lost in him. Every feeling I had for him flared to life, but I would be lying to myself if I said I fit into his life now.

"You can always come back here." She looks down sheepishly. "I know we were just acquaintances back then, but I remember the way Dagger looked at you. It was as if no one else in the room mattered. It still is."

I pause at that last part. I've been so out of it I'm just now getting my bearings and able to function. Certainly, I'm sore, but it's nothing near the pain I had before.

"Things with Cam"—I stop myself—"Dagger are so complicated." I look away, not allowing the hurt on my face to show. "And he has a woman." Whom he told me he was going to let loose.

Ma laughs. "Flash?" I don't respond. "They've had this fucked up kind of relationship for years. You need to talk to him about that." She pauses. "That is, if you want to stay."

Stay, here? The one place that I was so happy yet had so much pain?

"He doesn't need me here." He doesn't. He has a life. "Besides, I'm sure Tanner wants to head home, and I'm going with her." I let all the confidence I have come through my words.

"I understand wanting to be where your kids are, Mearna, but what if she wants to stay here, too?"

I've thought of that. The way she is with Rhys is like nothing I've ever seen. I've met every one of the guys she's dated, and not one of them had anything that Rhys does. To be honest, he scares the shit out of me, but when I really watch him with Tanner, it's like he changes. His hard is still there, but there is also some soft, only reserved for her. I appreciate that.

My biggest hang up is her being involved with this life. I stayed away for more than twenty years, trying to protect her from all of this, and now she's here, falling for her father's friend.

The age thing doesn't bother me. Maybe it should, but it's not on the top of my issue list. The top of that list is the biker life. It's not an easy life, and I didn't think I could hack it. While I know Tanner is strong and has spunk, I fear she wouldn't be able to handle it, either.

"Then I deal with it."

"You wouldn't talk her out of it, would you?" Ma asks.

"No. She has to lead her own life." I wouldn't make decisions for her. She's a grown woman and needs to make them for herself. As much as it would kill me to see her hurt, if that's the way this road lays, then I'll be there for her.

"You need to talk to Dagger," Ma says.

"I know. I got a call today that the funeral is in three days. Tanner and I need to go."

Ma sucks in a sharp breath. "You sure?"

"If we don't go, it'll look bad. I'm not sure what will happen when we get there, but Cam—Dagger said he took care of Griff and Miller, and I trust that he did." I do. No way would Dagger lie about something like that. I know he'll protect us.

"I'm sure he did."

Cooper, Ma's grandson, comes barreling into the room, a small airplane in hand as he flies it around us, making plane engine noises. He's adorable, and I totally get why everyone is so in love with the little guy.

"Whatcha doin'?" he asks, stopping by my chair.

I know I said I wouldn't think of the past, but my thoughts drift to Tanner at that age. Would she have been the apple in all these guys' eyes, winning the hearts of all of the women? How would she have turned out differently? How would having her father in her life have changed her? She's so beautiful and strong. I'm so damn proud of her for following her dream of being a hairstylist. I just can't help wondering what would be different.

What about me? Would I have been happy? Would I have grown into this life?

A nudge to my arm snaps me out of my thoughts. "Huh?"

Cooper giggles. "Whatcha doin'? Dreamin'?"

I give him a soft smile. "Yeah, something like that."

"You stayin'? I love my family," he says, and my heart breaks for Tanner. I denied her this family. Dammit.

Don't live in the past, Mearna! I chastise myself. *It does no good.*

"I'm not sure, little guy."

He smiles. "You should," he says before scampering off, resuming his airplane noises.

Why does life have to be so complicated?

17

RHYS

T ANNER'S ARMS WRAP AROUND ME TIGHTLY, HER HOT PUSSY against my ass. I made her wear my helmet, not taking a chance on hurting a hair on her head. Having her near me is the only thing calming me from the night's events. Not only did Dagger need the release, but I did, too. I should have killed the motherfucker.

I forget all thoughts and enjoy the ride with her arms squeezed around me. With the night surrounding us and very few cars on the road, I take my time enjoying this. I've never had a woman on the back of this thing, never thought I would. Now it all just feels right.

Fucking hell, I'm turning into one of those sappy fuckers.

A SOFT KNOCK comes to my bedroom door, waking me from sleep. Tanner's body is covering mine, her tits on my chest and legs entangled in mine. My hard dick rests on my abs and jumps at the sight of my girl.

The knock comes again. Son of a bitch.

"Sprite." I jostle her arm, and her eyes open slowly. "Gotta answer the door." She rolls off of me then reaches down to grab the blankets, shielding herself. Fuck, yeah, no motherfucker gets to see her. None. Those tits, ass, and pussy are mine, all fucking mine.

I roll out of bed and grab a pair of boxer briefs, slipping them on just as another knock sounds. My temper rises as I fling the door open.

Mearna jumps back in a gasp then groans from the sudden movement. Her eyes are wide and panicked.

"What's wrong?"

She takes in a deep breath. "You scared the shit out of me."

"Yeah, what do you need?"

"Mom?" Tanner's voice comes from behind me as she pushes her way in front of me. She now has on her jeans and shirt from last night.

Mearna eyes both of us under scrupulous observation. Let her.

"We have to head back. The funeral is in a couple of days, and we need to be there." The moment the words leave Mearna, Tanner's entire body stiffens. I'm not sure if it's the thought of going back or the thought of leaving. I should just tie her to my fucking bed and not let her go.

"Okay. We'll have to figure out a car," Tanner says, now all business, as if something clicked in her head. I love that shit about her. She sees a problem and takes hold of it.

"I'm going to talk to your father and see about borrowing one—" I cut Mearna off.

"I'll take care of it. You two get packed up, and I'll go talk to the brothers." I turn from the door, grabbing my jeans and pulling them over my hard erection.

"Mom, just give me a few, and I'll be down." I hear the soft click of the door and then, "Rhys?"

I turn as she flings off her shirt and opens her jeans, shimmying them down her body. My dick becomes painful in its confines. She is so fucking hot and sexy.

Tanner saunters up to me like one of those runway models, strutting with a sway in her step. She stops mere inches from me and gives me a soft kiss, pulling away before my hand reaches her head to deepen it. She then falls gracefully to her knees, looking up at me through her lashes. She undoes the button and zipper to my jeans before pulling them down to my ankles. The feel of her hands on me is indescribable.

"Sprite," I warn, but I think it's just for me. I'm not into letting chicks have control, but the spark in her eye and knowing that my dick will be in that hot, little mouth in a couple of seconds allows me to let her.

Her emerald eyes flutter as the curls of her hair fall down around her face. Her tiny hands reach into my boxers, pulling out my length. "Yes?" Her voice is completely seductive, and I know in that moment I'll never, not in a million years, have enough of this woman.

"Suck it." I can't help myself.

The triumphant smile on her face tells me she thinks she won, and for right now, I'm going with it.

Her pink tongue extends from her mouth and licks the underside of my dick, hitting the nerves running along the vein that is pulsing. Her hand grips firmly, much tighter than I would have thought, and she begins to stroke while she licks my head, slipping her tongue along the slit of my dick, taking a bit of time exploring there. I almost lose my load at the fucking sight, but I can't look away.

Tanner leans forward, and my dick is in heaven. The warmth of her mouth along with the wetness is a nirvana I've never experienced. Yeah, I've had my dick sucked by more women than I can count, but Tanner puts every fucking one of them to shame.

She moves up and down my dick, sucking in her cheeks then licking the head, over and over and over. While her hand still squeezes at my base, she pulls me as far as she can into the back of her throat, closing the muscles there, and I lose all sense of control.

I thread my fingers through her hair and begin pumping my dick in and out of her mouth. The sounds of wet flesh on flesh along with her occasional gasps for breath echo throughout the room, only spurring me on. My hips piston in and out. My balls draw up tight and a knowing tingle hits my spine.

"I'm going to fucking come, Sprite, and I want you to drink every fucking drop."

Her eyes lift to mine, want and need pulsating through them. That's the final nail as I come hard. Tanner swallows, but gets choked up for a moment before she quickly recovers. My come escapes her lips, falling down the corner of her mouth. Damn, that's hot.

She continues to stroke me even when my dick is soft and sated in her mouth. Then she sits back on her heels, allowing my dick to pop from her mouth, and swipes at my leftover come.

"My turn." I pick her up and toss her to the bed.

Opening up her legs, I find she's wet and ready for me. She starts to protest, but before the words come out, I'm on her fucking clit. She tastes as if heaven and hell mixed together to create this woman.

Tanner gasps and begins moving her hips, which I hold down, not allowing it any further. She mewls sexily as I attack the lips of her pussy, sucking them with everything I have.

Her clit sits out, ripe and ready. With flicks of my tongue, I get another hip jerk. I fucking love it. I toy with the nub just enough then pull it into my mouth as Tanner explodes around me, her cream filling my mouth in a rush. I take and saver it while continuing to pet her back down to earth.

Her body goes lax as I move up, kissing a path from her stomach to lips.

"Mornin'," I tell her as she smiles.

"Morning."

As much as I don't want to leave my bed with her in it, we have to.

"Got shit to do." I give her another deep kiss. "I'll go talk to the guys. You figure out you and your mom's stuff."

"Okay." Her voice is quiet with a touch of sadness creeping in.

I wrap my arms around her and pull her to my body. "You don't have to stay there," I tell her, not really having a clue what the fuck I'm doing, but it just feels like the right thing.

"Stay where?" she asks, burrowing into my neck, her arms around my back.

"There. Go to the funeral and come back here."

She pulls her head away and looks in my eyes. "This is just a fling, remember?" Her words piss me the fuck off, and I can feel my arms flex from them.

"Yeah." I pull her from my body and slap her ass, trying not to let the hurt of that sting.

She squeals and rushes to the bathroom, and I toss on my clothes.

"I'm going," I yell as I shut the door and try not to break it off its fucking hinges.

Why in the hell did I let that woman get under my fucking skin? I don't do that shit. Now she's probably leaving and not coming back. Fucking hell.

I turn to the wall and put my fist through the plaster, letting all my frustrations out. The drywall shatters from the impact, sending pieces floating around my hand, arm, and to the floor. I pull my hand out of the hole, not feeling any better whatsoever.

"WELL, THIS POSES A PROBLEM." Pops sighs at his desk, his hands latched behind his head as he leans from his chair. "Got a meeting with Ralphie. We're leaving in two hours."

I talked to Dagger, and we decided we should follow the girls up there in case anything came down on them. This puts a huge fucking wrench in that idea.

"We can send one of the prospects with them," Pops suggests and I growl.

With taking on Tug, Buzz and Breaker as full

members, we were had to get new Prospects, and there's only one I really trust.

"Derek." I demand. He helped us out during Blaze's kidnapping a while back. The other two are still too new to trust.

"I'm gonna send Dipstick, too."

It was Daggers turn to growl. "He's so damn timid I can't believe we are giving him a shot."

This is totally true. We voted to let him in because Pops said he saw something in him. I don't know what, and I'm still fucking looking.

"This will be good for him." Both Dagger and I nod, not liking it yet not going to change it, either. "After we meet with Ralphie, you can go meet up with your girls." Pops shakes his head. "Never thought I'd see the day Rhys."

"Me, either."

"And my fucking daughter." Dagger adds.

I smirk. "I'm the best fucking thing that happened to you ol' man."

He slaps me on the shoulder. "Remember you're an old man, too."

Who fucking cares? I'm older and don't give a rats ass what other people think, and Tanner doesn't seem to, either.

"Becs and I are going to meet with Ransom. Then we're taking off." Becs is the vice president of the club and a standup man. Ransom, on the other hand...

"What about?" I ask.

"Says he has some work for us. I'm just gonna go check it out." Pops shrugs.

"Want us to come along?" I trust no one but my brothers. I don't give a shit if Ransom has helped us out by helping us get even with people. He's not one of us.

"Nah. He just wants to go over some shit."

"All right. We're gonna get the girls off." Dagger says as we walk out the door.

"I'm coming as soon as we get our business done," I say to a misty-eyed Tanner. My woman's heart is pretty big.

"You don't need to. We'll be fine." I tap down the initial anger that wells inside. "You have a life here. Mine is up there." She shrugs as if it's all the same. Fuck no, it's not.

"I'll be there." I don't have time for a debate or any shit. I'm going, and that's that. This shit is final.

"Okay," she whispers as Dagger walks up. They really haven't had a chance to get to know each other. I feel a bit sad that she doesn't know yet what a great guy her father is.

"Take care of your mom. I'll be up there for the funeral."

Tanner nods, pain etched on her face as she tries to push it out. She's feeling the lack of connection between her and her father.

Dagger pulls her into his arms and hugs her as tears start to fall from her eyes. Dammit. Fucking tears, again. Dagger then kisses the top of her head and pulls away to her gasp.

"Go," he orders, but she turns to me.

She plows into my body hard, wrapping her arms around me.

"Sprite, it's only a couple of days."

She nods then pulls away. "Bye, Rhys."

Fuck, I feel like it's good-bye, good-bye. Fuck that.

"See you soon," I tell her, kissing her forehead before she gets in the car.

Both Dagger and I stare as the car and bikes holding Derek and Dipshit leave. Fucking hell.

I rip my fingers through my hair. I need to pound something, but I don't have time. We need to head out, too.

AFTER A FULL DAY on the road, only stopping to get some shut eye, we pull up to Ralphie's well-guarded compound. Stone walls line the front with wires across the top. We're out in the middle of no man's land with no one around for miles. Of course, Ralphie does have a very profitable business, and it needs to be protected.

The wide gates open as we pull up, Pops leading the way in our pack. We follow and are led to a side lot where an ape of a man points.

The place is huge, acres and acres with buildings here and there. Even houses are spread throughout with grassy areas included.

We park our bikes and kill the engines.

"This way," the ape calls out, and with a nod from Pops, we follow. The entire crew came on this one: Pops, Becs, Zed, Dagger, GT, Cruz, Buzz, Tug, Breaker, and myself. We even tagged the leftover prospect into driving the cage behind us, just in case.

The ape opens the door to a large warehouse and

goes through the doors where he stops us immediately. "Guns, cell phones, GPS's—whatever you've got needs to go into that bin right there." He points to a large plastic tote.

The idea of going into this shit unarmed does not sit right with me one bit. Luckily, it doesn't with Pops, either.

"We keep the guns and drop the cells," he says. The ape shakes his head, so Pops says, "Let me talk to Ralphie."

The ape pulls out his cell and holds it up to his ear. He has no hair and is built like a Mack truck. He then holds the phone out to Pops.

"What's going on, Ralphie?" Pops questions. "You know we need to have protection ... I understand." Pops's vein begins to tick in his neck, so whatever is being discussed over the phone isn't good. Fuck.

"Got it." He hands the phone back to the ape and addresses us. "Everything in the tub."

Fucking hell. We listen, taking all of our shit off and putting it in. Why the fuck do I feel like we are being lead to slaughter?

"We called this meeting. He has every right to have these precautions," Pops reasons, but even if they are valid, I don't give a flying shit.

After emptying out everything and going through a fucking metal detector, we are led to a large room where Ralphie sits at the head of the table with his goons behind him. The little balding man sits prominently while he waits for us to sit down.

"You seem to have caused me a huge problem," Ralphie says, his fingers steepled, a clear sign of power.

"Those assholes were trying to take one of ours," Pops replies coolly.

"From what I understand, she was already theirs to begin with."

From the corner of my eye, I see Tug's hands fist, but he holds his shit together.

"So they thought. She didn't feel the same way," Pops says.

Ralphie smiles sinisterly. "Let's cut the shit. I don't have time for it. I do not have a problem in this situation. My pockets are fully lined, and the product is the same as usual."

So, those fuckers that took over paid Ralphie to keep him off their backs. They were smarter than I gave them credit for.

"You, on the other hand, have a problem. What do you want from me?"

This blows more than I realized. We owe him, but if we keep to our end, he'll stick to his.

"Get them off our asses," Pops says simply.

"And how do you propose I do that?" Ralphie questions.

"Threaten to pull your product if they don't."

Ralphie laughs. This time, it's real. "You think coming here and doing this grand bullshit will get me to roll over?"

"Seems you have some rats in your organization," Pops says.

It takes everything in my gut to keep my face impassive. How in the fuck did I miss this shit?

"Buzz here pulled up some information that I'm sure you want, because it's a Fed."

My spine stiffens. It's fucking painful to keep still.

"You're lying. My guys wouldn't," Ralphie says.

Pops's gaze turns to a guy with reddish-brown hair who stands to the left of Ralphie. His posture is stiff, but in control. His hands are clasped in front of him as he stares straight ahead.

"Isn't that right, Agent Peterson?" Pops asks.

It's small, so fucking small I'm not sure anyone saw it, but his left eye gives a slight twitch to the name. Son-of-a-bitch.

"Levi." Ralphie turns to the man, and Pops chuckles.

"Try Samuel David Peterson, FBI undercover. I'd appreciate it if you checked him for wires, considering this meeting and all." Pops leans back in the chair. This right here is why he is our leader.

"Dez," Ralphie orders another guy, who goes over to the agent, taking the gun away from him.

"I don't know what these assholes are talking about," the agent snaps.

"Check him," Ralphie orders then narrows his gaze at Pops. "Where's the proof?"

Pops looks over to Buzz who nods, reaching into his vest and pulling out a manila folder. He slides it across the table to Ralphie who opens it. He rustles through the papers, and whatever he sees turns his eyes to the venom of a snake.

"Gut him," he calls out. "Get a sweep of the entire place." His words are dripping in anger so thick, if we weren't sitting, it may have just knocked us on our asses.

They carry the agent out of the room, kicking and swearing that he didn't do anything. Whatever is in Ralphie's hand must be some doozy of evidence.

"What else?" Ralphie asks Pops.

"There are two more. They aren't in this room, though." This time, Pops pulls out a manila envelope, setting it in front of him. "I give you this, and you take care of our problem."

"You're fucking lucky you're a top runner for me." Ralphie shakes his head. "I clear this, and you do a run for me."

Pops's eyes narrow, the tension in the room growing tight. "What kind of run?"

"I have some precious cargo that needs to make its way to Southern Texas. You deliver it and give me the envelope, and we call it even."

As much as I fucking don't want to run whatever it is, it's in our best interest to get these assholes off our backs and for there to be a clean slate.

Pops looks to each of us at the table as we each nod in agreement. It's not like we have a huge choice at the moment. It's either this or pay out two hundred K. We have to trust that he will follow through.

"Fine," Pops says, sliding the paper across the table. "What are we taking?"

18

___

TANNER

I PULLED MYSELF TOGETHER ONCE WE WERE ON THE ROAD. Mom and I talked the entire way, but I avoided questions about Rhys, not knowing what exactly to say. He's not a one woman kind of man, and I can't have that. Our arrangement was for the time I was there. When I left, it was over. The thought of another woman in his bed brings me to my knees, crushing my heart with a sledge-hammer. Therefore, I don't want to talk about him. I want to avoid the subject.

I have this gut feeling he won't be showing up for the funeral today or anytime else, for that matter. That feeling depresses the hell out of me. That's why the good-bye was so hard. I knew he ruined me for other men, and there is no going back from him. Even if by some miracle he does come up, he won't stay. His life is there. Mine and my mother's lives are here.

I slip into the black dress and put on my pumps. We arrived back at my apartment late last night. I gave Mom my bed and slept on the couch. She says she has to do paperwork tomorrow for the house. It's a good thing she owned it because they weren't officially married, and she would have gotten nothing on the insurance. At least, that's what the guy told her on the phone on the way up here.

My stomach is twisting like a roller coaster on crack. I know it's a combination of today's events and the fact that I haven't heard a word from Rhys, only proving to me further that we are done and over with.

The ache in my heart has nothing to do with the death of James. To him, good-riddance. The pain is solely for Rhys. I'm not saying we'll have some happily ever after, but more time would have been nice.

I'll see if he shows up today then figure out what Mom and I are going to do.

I walk into the living room where Mom sits on the couch, her head back as she looks up at the ceiling. Her marks have mainly healed, and I did her makeup liberally to hide anything else. She's wearing a back pencil skirt; flowing, black shirt; and black flats.

"You ready?" I ask, moving closer to the couch.

She turns her head my way. "As much as I can be."

STARES.

All around me, people turn to look at me and my mother. She's doing her bit as the grieving widow, but I have to admit I'm pretty sure most of her tears are very real. Several mourners, including James's parents, hugged us when we arrived as we took our seats.

The service is a full-out cop's funeral with cars

following the hearse while I drive my mother behind it. She was asked to ride in the limo with the parents, but declined, saying she wanted to be alone. I don't really know her reasoning, but I went with it.

As I stand here at the reception with cops every-where, I can't help looking every few minutes to see if Rhys has shown up. I've checked my phone hundreds of times, only to be disappointed each time. Still nothing.

I've talked to so many cops and well-wishers, smiling and shaking hands, even accepting hugs when they offered them.

It's so strange that the reason all these people are joined together is because I took the man's life. Me. He deserved it—don't get me wrong—but that is still on my shoulders. I've done my best to hide any emotion the entire time.

What I wouldn't give to have Rhys's arms around me to take it all away, but he's not here and, with the funeral coming to an end, not coming. I knew it, but a small part of me hoped, and now I feel incredibly let down.

"Ms. O'Ryan?" The voice has me turning quickly without thinking.

"Officer Miller." I need to work on masking myself better. Seeing him dredges up everything that happened back in Sumner, even the fact that Griff didn't show for his best friend and partner's funeral. I want to know what they did, but I don't. I think it would be best if I didn't.

"So sorry for your loss." A very pretty, petite blonde stands next to him, clutching his hand like she's afraid he'll vanish.

"Thank you," I respond, the words coming out light.

"Officer Miller, thank you so much for coming," my

mother says from next to me, extending her hand like everything that happened has just vanished into thin air. She's so poised and perfect. I want to be her.

I have to hand it to the man; he's very good at nonchalance. He introduces us to his very quiet wife, and then they skirt off. I heave a breath after he leaves. I need a moment.

"I'm going to the bathroom," I tell my mother, moving off quickly.

I enter the stall and sit to do my business, checking my phone again. A giddy rise comes out of me when it shows I have a missed text, though it's from my father's phone, not Rhys's. I try not to let the disappointment swirl inside of me, but it's hard.

I open up the little envelope on my phone.

THIS IS **R. Got club business. Can't make it. Phone dead. Will call soon.**

HOW IS it possible to have such a barrage of emotions knocking me on my ass at one time? I'm so happy he contacted me yet so disappointed that I'm not going to see him.

I type out a message.

OKAY. **Miss you.**

I STARE AT THE WORDS. *No, don't put that.* I erase the last two words and send it. At least I know for sure so no more looking over my shoulder, hoping to see him.

I put my phone in my clutch and finish, coming out of the stall to wash my hands. I stop abruptly when Griff's wife looks at me in the mirror, her eyes red-rimmed. I've met her a couple of times, but I'm nowhere near friends with her. My nerves pick up just a bit.

Suzie turns to me. "I'm so sorry for your loss." A fresh batch of tears fall from her eyes as she sniffles and moves away from the sink.

"Thank you."

I let Suzie lead this conversation since I don't know what happened to Griff and don't want to say anything wrong.

"I'm sorry I'm such a mess. I haven't heard from Griff for days. He said he was going out on a fishing trip, but I haven't heard from him. I called down to Georgia where he said he was going, and they haven't found him. I'm so scared."

Okay, so he didn't come home. Chances are, he's dead, and good-riddance to him, as well.

"I'm so sorry to hear that."

"You were in Georgia. Did you see him?"

My throat dries, and I feel the room closing in on me. Shit.

"Georgia is a very big place," I respond, not lying in the least.

Her hand comes out and clutches my arm. "I'm so scared. I ..." Fresh tears coat her eyes, and the pit of my stomach drops for this woman. She loves the asshole, and chances are, she'll never see him again. And I'm okay with that. I'm actually okay that this woman is crying for a man who put his hands on me. What in the hell is wrong with me?

She bats away the wetness and blots her face with tissues. "I'm sorry. You have enough on your plate. Griff loved James so much."

You have no idea. "I know he did." I rinse my hands quickly, knowing I have sanitizer in my purse. I need to get out of here. "I have to go find my mom."

"Oh, sure, dear. Thanks for listening."

I haul ass out to my mom. I thank the clock on the wall that tells me this is almost over.

"Mom." I bend down to her ear and whisper, "We need to go." I'm hoping to convey that I'm just done. I've had my fill and need to retreat to somewhere far, far away.

Mom nods and rises from the chair, excusing herself from the table of people I've met yet can't remember their names.

Mom says her good-byes with me next to her, smiling and nodding the entire time. Walking up to James's parents, my stomach starts churning.

"Mearna, darling," James's mother Rose says, the stench of her floral perfume filling the space. My mother goes willingly into her arms, hugging her back. "I know this probably isn't the time, but we talked to the lawyer. He has a will that James filed, leaving everything he has to you, including his pension."

I grasp my mom's hand, not knowing exactly what that means, but I know it's good.

"He also said that the insurance company is investigating, but the police have already closed, saying it was an accidental fire. You should be able to get the recovery of it."

I want to say, *yes, because she owns the house,* but maybe his parents don't know that tidbit of information. Therefore, I keep my lips shut. I just want the hell out of here.

"I have an appointment tomorrow with the insurance company in hopes of getting things sorted," she says.

"I heard you met your father." Tim, James's father, looks at me. His gaze is expectant.

"Yes," I answer.

"That's awfully nice," Tim says, looking at my mother. "Strange, the timing."

I don't move an inch as my mother squeezes my hand. "Tanner has been asking for quite some time. I am absolutely devastated about James." She plays it off. My mother is officially the shit. Yes. The. Shit.

"Sure you are, honey." Rose pats my mother's arm.

Tim tilts his head, and I meet him stare for stare. It's like he's looking inside of me or something. Go for it. I don't waver a bit, and he is the first to look away. Relief fills me. I have learned from my mother, and I like that a lot.

My mother wastes no time getting us the hell out of there.

———

I SHUT the door to the apartment and plop my purse on the floor along with my keys.

"Bad day?" my mother asks.

I move to the couch and lie down a bit dramatically,

but that's how I feel at the moment: pissed, hurt, alone, slapped in the face ... I can go on.

"Went to see Anderson. He replaced me at the shop and no longer needs my services, or so he says." I lost my job, even though I used some of my vacation time. "He said that, since I didn't call him to tell him what was going on, he just replaced me."

"Did you tell him that James died?" Mom asks, coming to sit in the chair next to the couch.

"Yep. He said he was sorry, but that was it. He hired this blonde bimbo with tits so huge she needs two bras to hold them up. And get this, she calls him sir. What the hell is that about?" I grind out and Mom chuckles. "This isn't funny. I have no money!"

"Sweetheart, calm down. First of all, we have plenty of money. The insurance payoff is on its way, and I have plenty to hold us over. Second, if she is calling him sir in that sense, be happy that you're not her." She laughs more.

She's right. I've read enough books and watched enough movies to know where she is going with this. Still, I loved that job. It was an awesome place to work at.

"I got a call from your father while you were gone."

Five days, and all I've gotten from Rhys was a text, short and clipped. He never called like he said he was going to, and I for sure wasn't going to call him. Screw that. All right, I'm probably being a little overdramatic, but it's better this way. He's splitting off, and it's for the best. Nowhere in his text did he say he was on his way here. As a matter of fact, he said he couldn't make it due to club business, so I know that must be more important. Then again, like Princess said, all club business is more important. I shouldn't resent that, yet I do. It gave Rhys the perfect escape.

The fact that my father called my mother is a bit baffling, though.

"I didn't know you two were talking."

"We talk quite a bit."

So, Dagger can call my mother and talk, but Rhys can't call me. A lead weight hangs in my gut. What if the reason he hasn't is because he's seeing other women? Since the arrangement is over, he decided he needed sex from others. The lead rolls in my stomach as bile starts to rise in my throat. He can't be, and if he is, I don't want to know about it.

"Really?"

"Their business took a little longer, but he said he'll be here in a couple of days."

I chew my bottom lip, wanting to ask if Rhys is coming, wanting to know if he already forgot about me. I don't, though. I hardly ever speak to my mother about him. It's like, if I don't talk about it, then it's not real.

"Then what?" I ask.

"Sweetheart, we need to decide if we want to say here or move down to Sumner."

I focus on her and gape. "You want to move there?"

"I don't have much up here besides you."

"I'll have to think about it." After all, if things are truly done with Rhys, I sure as hell don't want to live in the same area as him or see him around my father. I know me, and that would be too much for me to bear. "And what is going on with you and Dagger? He has a woman, you know."

My mother's eyes shut as if the pain is too much to

take. I understand her. The thought of the man you care about being with another is too much.

"I know. I'm not sure about anything at the moment." She shifts in the chair and lays her head back, looking at the ceiling.

Times like these, I wish I could read my mother's thoughts. Hell, I wish my thoughts were more understandable.

19

RHYS

"You call my daughter yet?" Dagger asks as we stop for food on our journey back to Sumner.

Fucking Ralphie. This trip shouldn't have taken this long, but the catch to the deal was pickups, several of them throughout the US on the way. Stupid fucker. At least now the debt is settled. He just needs to hold up his end of this deal.

"I'll get to it," I tell him, taking a bite of the nasty-ass burger, needing something in my stomach.

"I'm going back for Mearna," Dagger tells me.

"Are you?"

"Fuck, yes. That's my woman," he says with absolute confidence. I'm glad he knows what the hell he wants. "When Mearna comes, Tanner's coming, too."

"Good," I tell him, taking another bite and washing it down with a soda.

Do I want Tanner? Fuck, yes, but I gotta be straight. Never in my forty-something years have I ever had only one woman for any period of time. While her pussy is the best I've ever had, I'm not sure I have enough confidence in myself to stick to only hers. I've never had to. Tanner told me flat-out she wasn't that type, but for her, I want to try. Fucking hell.

"I'll head up with ya."

"You sure about that?" he questions.

I know he's right. My dick has seen so many pussies and mouths in its time. For Tanner, though, I will do my damnedest.

On a couple of our stops, I had the opportunity to get fucked and sucked by road bunnies, and I turned them down, each one of them. That was a fucking first. I've never turned down free pussy, but I did because of Tanner, because it's her mouth I want wrapped around my cock. Yeah, I'll definitely try.

"Yep, let's get the fuck out of here," I tell him as the brothers grab their bikes, and we ride off.

"FUCKING HATE that my girl lives here," Dagger says, climbing up the stairs. I agree.

"Let's just get them home." *And I'll see what happens from there.*

Dagger pounds on the door, and a beat later, it opens just a touch. Tanner's emerald eyes peek around the door and focus on Dagger. The door flies open as she wraps her arms around him with some kind of screech thing that I may need to replace my ear drum for.

"You're here!" she says as Mearna comes to the door.

"Yep, brought someone with me."

Tanner stills and looks around her father. Her eyes

well up with tears when she sees me. Well, hell, isn't that something? I can say that, throughout my entire life, I've never had a woman cry because she was happy to see me.

Dagger steps into the apartment just as Tanner flings herself at me, wrapping her arms and legs around me securely. I cup her ass, holding her up, the heat of her pussy hitting me hard. I haven't fucked since the last time I saw her, and I fucking need it badly.

Her lips collide with mine as her tears hit my face in droplets. She really didn't think I would come, did she? I can't blame her, though. With all the shit that Princess filled her with, I'm surprised her lips are attached to mine. Still, I greedily take everything she's giving me.

"You want to come in?" Mearna says from the side of us as she looks around outside. I don't give a shit who's fucking looking. There's no way I'm detaching from these lips.

I continue to kiss her, carrying her directly to the bedroom and kicking the door shut with my boot. I take her hard and fast, leaving us both breathless.

"I LIKE THESE." I bounce one of Tanner's curls in my hand.

She's lying naked, sprawled out on top of me, her heat keeping me warm against the coolness of her apartment.

"I was having one of those girl days," she says as if I know what in the hell a girl day is. Whatever. She looks fucking gorgeous.

"Didn't think I'd come?" I ask, needing to get it out there and over with.

"Not really. You're not that guy, Rhys. I thought you'd be done with me."

My gut feels heavy as I pull her lips to mine. "No, not done. We're just getting started. Come move to Sumner." Her eyes widen. "I'm not perfect by a long shot, but I want you."

I'm not giving this shit up.

Can't.

Won't.

"How do I know that we'll last? And for how long? A day, a week? This is a huge change for me."

The instant her words hit my brain, I know what I need to do. I need to only be with her. It's new, different, but fuck, I don't want anyone else.

"I know we'll work. There's no other woman for me. It's only you, Sprite."

She smiles, and I get closer, brushing my lips against hers.

"Only you," I whisper.

"Okay," she whispers back, and I feel like I've won the fucking lottery.

PACKING the women up wasn't a hard task. Mearna already had most of her things together from her travels down to Sumner. She agreed right away when Tanner and I came out to talk. She and Dagger were in an embrace that made Tanner still in my arms, no doubt in shock. She was able to pull herself together, though.

Tanner only had a few things she wanted, and by the

next day, we were on our way to Sumner, following behind them.

———

"IT'S SETTLED. The assholes are backing off with the cash, and we are in the clear," Pops says as we sit around the table at church. "Ralphie laughed his ass off after I chewed him out for all the stops. I'm guessing he did it on purpose to be a fucking asshole."

"Figures," Dagger grunts.

I nod in response.

"Buzz, tell me you've got something." Pops directs his eyes to the man we are counting on.

"I've narrowed it down." He looks around the room. "They are here in Georgia."

"You have got to be shitting me!" GT explodes, rising from his seat. "Who the fuck is it? This shit has to end *now*."

"We all agree, son," Pops says calmly. "Sit down and let's hear him out."

GT listens, sitting back down, the glare still in his gaze.

"I don't have much, just narrowed some of the data transmitters to here, but the state is fucking huge." Buzz sweeps his hand through his hair. "I'm getting closer, though."

That man has been working around the clock for days on cracking the computers. He deserves a hell of a fucking party once this shit is done.

"All right. What about our buddies Griff and Miller?"

Pops asks, looking at Dagger and myself. Considering neither one of us were there, I'm not sure why.

I shrug.

"Griff should be found any day now, about two hundred miles from here. I have eyes on Miller. He hasn't said a word," Becs answers.

"Tanner said she saw Miller, and there was nothing. Said she also talked to Griff's wife who was distraught, but nothing has come back on them for the fire or for the ass's disappearance," I include.

"Sounds good. Let's get out of here." Pops slams the gavel.

"Come on." I grab Tanner's hand and pull her out the door of the two bedroom apartment that she insisted on getting with her mother. She's only been here a few days, but it was the first thing she insisted on. I wanted to lock her ass up at my place about three miles from here; however, she didn't agree. I don't know why I let her have a choice in the matter. Regardless, it won't be long before I get her where I want her. If she's here in Sumner, I want her in my fucking bed, but for now, being in hers works fine.

"Where are we going?" she asks as I pull her to my bike and hand her the helmet, which she puts on with a smile on her face.

"It's a surprise."

"You know I love being on the back of your bike," she tells me as she throws her leg over and nestles behind me.

"Good thing, because I love you being back there, too."

She gasps. I only say what comes natural, and at that moment, that did.

She squeezes me as we pull off for a ride.

The day is beautiful: not too hot, not too cold, just fucking perfect. The wind around us while Tanner's wrapped around my body is the best fucking place in the world. I honest to God don't think I'll ever get enough of her.

We ride for hours, taking back roads as I show her around Sumner and the surrounding area. I want her to see her new home and show her the places that I've loved going to over the years. As we pass by places, I tap her arm and point to them, and she just nods her head. I'll explain everything to her later.

I pull the bike up to my place. It's nothing big, only a three bedroom log cabin that I bought as soon as I could afford it. I never had a home before this one. I helped a few buddies of mine build it. A lot of blood, sweat, and beer went into making the place, and I wouldn't change it for the world. It sits back on two acres with woods around it. It's serene and quiet. While I love being at the club, it does get to be a bit much at times. When I need some time, I come here.

I've brought Tanner here a couple of times, but we have never really stayed long. With getting her and her mother settled, it's been hectic. Hopefully, things will calm the hell down now. That's why we're here today. I want to show her something.

I park the bike, and Tanner climbs off. She pulls off

the helmet and flings her blondish red hair. Fuck, that's hot.

I pull her to me and lay a searing kiss on her lips. Nope, never getting enough.

I lace our fingers together. "Come with me." I pull her around the back of the house and through the small path in the woods.

She follows, the swish of her boots on the grass right behind me.

I pause when I see it through the clearing, and Tanner inhales deeply.

"Oh, my God," she whispers.

I smile. I'm so fucking proud of this place. "I built it. It took me a couple of years, but I think it turned out great."

She pulls away from my hand and moves up the small stairs and into the grand gazebo I created by myself. It's not small. No, I had to knock out trees and make a huge clearing for it, but with the cedar boards, I made it into a huge octagon, incasing it with railing all around.

"This is beautiful, Rhys." Her eyes are wide as she takes everything in.

There is a large, wooden swing that hangs in one area; a grill built into the structure; and a hammock swings freely on one of the railing sides. The huge area in the middle has couches, chairs, and even a small fire pit. I added a hole in the top of the roof that can open and close when I have it on, which if I have to be honest, isn't much. I hardly ever get to come out here.

"You did all of this?" she asks, dragging her fingers over the fabric cushions of the couch.

"Yep. I don't get to come out here as much as I'd like, but it's peaceful." I walk over and snag her arm. "Sit."

We both take a spot on the couch, facing the fire pit that isn't lit. I wrap my arm around the back of the cushion and pull her to me. She feels so damn right, so perfect when she snuggles her body up against mine.

We sit there for long moments in silence. I kick my feet up on the small table I made out of the leftover cedar and just enjoy life for the moment. Tanner shifts, getting comfortable, and then I rest my cheek on the top of her head. This right here is what's missing in my life. Then it hits me like a ten ton boulder, and I feel my body tighten.

My heart begins to pick up, and all of a sudden, my body is extremely hot. My mouth goes dry, and my grip tightens on Tanner. She's what I've been missing. Her. Tanner. She's it for me. This ... This is going to be my life from this point on—my club and my girl.

The tightness recedes, and something foreign takes its place. I don't want to call it love, because I don't believe I'm capable of that shit, but it's something. The feeling is euphoria, and I fucking love it.

I suck in deeply, and Tanner hesitantly raises her hand cupping the side of my face. I try not to flinch, but I do a bit. She doesn't stop and I suck in deep something inside of me not allowing myself to back down from this. Tanner wouldn't hurt me and I need to trust in that. I haven't talked to her about my past because that is where I want to leave it. I need to look to the future.

"Are you okay?" she asks, but I can't answer, from the touch to the swirling emotions squeezing my insides tight. I can't.

I need to show her. I have to show her how much she means to me. I may not be able to say the words, because

I don't fully understand it, but my gut is compelling me to show her.

I lay my hand on top of hers then guide her to my lips. Sparks combust as our lips touch. I've never done sweet before, ever. I can't help worrying that I'll fuck this up somehow, but I go with my gut and let it lead.

Tanner moves and straddles my hips, her hands coming to my face, and I freeze for a moment, saying nothing, then go back to kissing her.

I want her to touch me. I want her to claim me as hers. I want her to inflame me.

Her hot heat rests on my already aching dick as both her hands cup my face, and she takes every opportunity to touch me. I have to admit, that shit is getting me off.

I take my time exploring her sexy as hell mouth, memorizing each and every sound she makes when I touch her in different places. I've never thought kissing a woman could be so damn powerful. With each movement of her lips, though, I can't get enough.

"Need you," I tell her, and she nods then stands up for me.

I slowly pull down her jeans, kissing her legs as I go, loving the feel of her shudders from my touch. I remove them as she lifts her feet for me, and then I rise, taking another mouthwatering kiss before I step back.

I slip my hands under my shirt, but her hand stops me.

"Let me," she says softly as she lifts the fabric from my body. Her nails trace down my chest as she makes her way to my jeans next. "You are so sexy." She unbuttons my jeans and removes everything from the waist down.

My dick bounces on my abs, hard and ready, and my blood pumps as she rises enticingly.

Wrapping my arm around her waist, I lift her, kiss her, and then lay her down on the couch. As I settle my hips between her legs, her foot comes to rest on my ass while I devour her in another searing kiss, trying to pour into her the words that I'm not saying.

I place my dick at her entrance where the heat is detrimental. I realize quickly I have no condom on. Fuck. I reluctantly pull away to go to my pants and take care of that, repositioning myself.

I lace our fingers together and place them above her head. Entering her is heaven, but I go so slowly, so fucking slowly I'm sure I'm going to make myself crazy.

I make myself hold back, gliding in and out of her heat, building us both up slow and steady as we kiss with everything we have.

I pull away and look into Tanner's beautiful emerald eyes.

"Rhys?" she says questioningly.

I'm not sure what look I'm giving her, but she can tell this is different than the other times. This is special.

Instead of answering, I kiss her.

She rips her mouth away. "Oh, God," she yells, cutting my restraint.

I continue to hold her hands as I thrust harder and deeper, wanting to climb inside of her and claim her for the world to see. Her orgasm hits, squeezing my dick within an inch of its life, and I explode while looking into her eyes.

It's the best fucking experience I've ever had, and it was with her. My woman.

20

TANNER

I LIE IN RHYS'S ARMS, ALLOWING MY HEART TO COME TO terms with what just happened. I've fucked him enough times to know what just happened was something way more than that. It felt as if he were making love to me— sweet, lustful, unconditional love. It's strange because part of me is right there with him, while the other is scared as hell. I need to get over that, but how when your man has the reputation of screwing lots of other women?

I'm not that experienced, but I don't think I'm bad in bed. Rhys seems satisfied enough. What scares me is not being enough for him. What if he needs more than what I can give him?

His actions as of late show me every moment that he's thinking of no one but me. I need to go with that and hope that he takes care *with* me.

"You're thinking awfully hard there," he grumbles low as he strokes my hair while I lie on his chest, listening to the rise and fall of his breaths. Each puff helps to sooth my wayward thoughts.

"A lot to think about," I tell him. It's probably not the best time to get into some deep conversation when we're both completely sated and in our own little worlds.

"Talk to me." I close my eyes briefly at his command.

"Is this real, Rhys? I want this to be real." I speak with every bit of honesty, pain, and uncertainty pouring from each syllable.

He shifts us so our eyes are level, and he's holding me tightly to the couch so I don't fall. I wrap my arms around him and hold on. His eyes dance, making all the tough, scary lines of his face soften. I'm certain not many people get to see this side of Rhys, and I'm ecstatic to be one of them.

"It's about as real as it gets," he says as his eyes tell me he's in this the same way I am. "It can't get any closer, Sprite."

I kiss him with every bit of emotion I'm feeling, and he deepens it. My heart flutters and twists in my chest. I feel it. It's smacking me in the face. Rhys is mine.

"RHYS, I need to get a job, and this is perfect," I tell him, my hand cocked on my hip and foot pointing out, going all bitch on him.

"I don't want you working there." He crosses his arms over his chest and widens his stance. It's scary, but I'm not backing down. I've been looking for a job around here for the past week, and there is nothing. I refuse to mooch off my mother. I have to support myself.

"Princess upped security, and I'll be working behind

the curtain. They'll have to get through bouncers to get back to me," I try to reason with him.

When Princess offered me the job, at first I didn't think she was serious. Yeah, I helped out there once, but I thought she was just being nice. As time went on, however, she started pursing me harder, and I finally said yes.

"I don't give a shit. Remember what happened?"

Do I ever.

"Yes, and it won't happen again," I retort. "I think it'll be a lot of fun."

Princess wants me to style the girls' hair before they go on stage, but on top of that, she wants me to color and cut each of them once a month. She is also offering me almost three times as much money as my other job, and it's shorter hours. I'd only be there for their initial dance, and then I'm gone.

"Fuck!" he growls, swiping his hands through his hair in frustration. "I should just paddle your ass."

"Rhys, it's a job. I'll hardly be there, and she's paying me a shit load. You've gotta give this to me." I move closer to him and grab the front of his shirt. Some of the starch comes out of his spine as he sucks in a breath.

"I can't be there to keep those fuckers in line. You have to carry a gun."

While I should be shocked and mortified at this request, I'm not. Over this past week, I learned that everyone in the club carries, including Princess, Blaze, and Casey, whom I met briefly.

"Only if you teach me." I don't have the first clue what to do with a gun, let alone how to load and fire it. Yeah, no clue. I'm fine with learning, though.

"Fine," he growls, pulling me into him. His hand comes to the top of my head, and he kisses me on my temple. "If any of those fuckers touch a hair on your head, I'll fucking kill them."

At that, I smile. I've grown to like his overprotective side ... to a point. He tries to get more and more, but I still have a spine, and I've made sure he knows that. A prime example is this current conversation.

"Okay, babe," I tell him, burying my face in his neck and inhaling. I love being this close to him. I just can't get enough.

"And I'm fucking talking to Princess. I want someone on you the whole time. I don't give a shit if I have to put a prospect on you for when I can't be there. I fucking will."

I hold onto him more tightly.

"I CANNOT BELIEVE you hooked up with Rhys," Casey says from the seat next to me while we converse in the clubhouse. "And look at him."

My eyes cut to him. He stands with his legs apart, the corded muscles of his arms crossed while a beer dangles from his fingers. His face is hard as he listens to whatever Dagger, Cruz, and GT have to say.

"What?" I ask, not seeing anything truly wrong. He looks pissed, but when does he not?

"No, look at the couch." She points over as a club momma eyes Rhys up and down, not taking her stare off him for a moment. She wets her lips as she rises from the seat. My heart picks up as the woman saunters over to him, her hips swaying way too much to be considered normal. I want to get up and stop whatever is going to happen. My gut tells me to sit and watch, while my heart tells me I should guard it.

Her fingers graze his arm, and I clench my hands. She has her hands on him. Fury, the same as when I saw my mother's battered up body, hits me hard. It takes everything in me to keep my ass planted in the seat.

"This'll be good," Princess says, sitting back in her chair and eyeing the show.

Rhys turns to the woman and lifts his chin, and my heart plummets. Is he inviting her? Is he welcoming her touch? No, he can't be.

His attention goes back to the conversation, but the woman keeps going. Her hands now go to his shoulders as she leans into him, brushing her fat, fake breasts over his arm. A hand comes to my leg and squeezes hard.

I turn to Princess. "What?" I grit out through my teeth.

"Just wait," she tells me, but all of my insecurities rise to the surface, making me want to punch something. I could just reach behind my back and pull out the small gun Rhys taught me to shoot a couple of weeks ago. I could blast her right in the head since I have a killer shot.

I shake my head. Listen to me. I sound like a vigilante, like I would really take a life for touching the guy I'm sleeping with. Well, practically living with, considering he's either at my place or we're at his every night. I see what he meant with not getting an apartment, but I needed that with my mother.

I breathe out deeply and try to tamp down all the raging thoughts. However, when she stands on her tiptoes and whispers something in his ear, something breaks inside of me. It's not my heart; it's my fury.

Princess's grip tightens on me just as I'm about to rise. I want to ignore it, but her grip is pretty strong, not allowing me to do that.

Rhys has a sour expression on his face as he steps back from the woman. "Get the fuck off me," he growls loudly enough the whole room can hear. "See that woman?" He points over to me, his eyes meeting mine as a smirk plays on his lips from whatever he sees on my face. He turns back to the woman. "That's my woman."

Her eyes flitter to me, and her top lip curls up. "So? You always love to play, and I'm horny," she whines.

That's it. The straw has broken the camel's back. I rise, shrugging off the clamping hand on my leg, my chair falling to the ground I'm so quick. I stalk up to the woman who has her intentions on my man. His eyes find mine, brimming with humor.

I tap the woman on the shoulder, and she turns then sneers when she sees me.

"Back the hell off," I tell her, getting right up in her face that is covered with way too much makeup than should be allowed.

"I get it. You're here, and he can't play." She rolls her eyes.

Before I think better of it, my arm comes back, and I land a hard right hook to the woman's cheek. I've never been a fighter, but after James and the assholes at X, I got over it.

The woman's head snaps to the side as her hand comes up to her face just as she falls to her knees on the floor.

"I said back the hell off," I tell her, standing over her body, her eyes wide.

I know I don't look like the type to lay a bitch out, but looks can be deceiving. My eyes move up to Rhys who has a full-out smile on his face.

"And you," I tell him, pointing my finger in his chest. "I told you I wouldn't put up with that shit."

I turn to head back toward the table where Casey and Princess have big smiles, but a steel arm comes around my waist and lifts me off the ground. I wiggle from Rhys's strong hold, but he doesn't allow me to get away. He says nothing, only walks straight back to his room at the clubhouse amidst all the cheers and whistles behind us.

The door slams, and suddenly, my front is pressed to the door, his hot breath at my ear. "Sprite, that was the hottest fucking thing I've ever seen."

Briefly, I have the thought, *That was the hottest thing you've seen? What the hell?* But whatever. Instead, I focus on my body coming alive under his touch.

"I'm gonna check your hand ... after I fuck you." He undoes my jeans, and they, along with my underwear, are gone in a flash.

"I'm gonna fuck you so hard every motherfucker in this place will know who you belong to."

Wetness pools down below, and without him even touching my clit, it quivers in anticipation.

"I'm putting my fucking rag on you, too, so no one mistakes it."

Excitement like no other spikes through me as the sounds of his zipper and rustle of his jeans dropping echo over our heavy pants.

He lifts my leg, bending it at the knee as the blunt tip

of his erection nudges my opening. Without mercy, he slams into me, and I cry out from the invasion, but the burn turns to pleasure in a flash.

I find it hard to breathe as I try to clutch the door, finding nothing but a flat surface. He presses me harder against it. He must have sensed I was slipping as he continues his thrusts.

This isn't sweet or caring. No, this is hot, hard, and carnal. And I love it.

The pressure burns inside me as his length awakens every nerve, sending me soaring in no time. I scream his name and suck in deep breaths as he continues until he finds his release with a large grunt.

I sag against the door, his arm dropping my leg and wrapping around me to support me. If it weren't there, I would for sure fall into a tumble on the ground.

He stays inside of me while we catch our breath, the hot tickle of his breath coming through my shirt at my back. Damn, that was hot.

21

DAGGER

WHY DID I THINK FLASH WOULD JUST PACK HER SHIT AND leave again? I knew better. I also knew better than to call her ass over the phone and break shit off. I've been with the woman so long I should have done it face to face, but in the moment, all I could think about was taking Mearna home to my house that I bought. In other words, I was leading with my dick and not my fucking head. Stupid, but I did this shit to myself.

I walk through what was my very well-put-together home, especially since Flash kept shit picked up and took good care of it. Now the once kickass living room is torn to shreds, and I mean that literally. The bitch took a fucking knife to my brown leather couches and chairs. It looks like a hammer or sledgehammer, for that matter, went to work on my coffee tables and my fucking flat screen. Particles of wood and glass litter the hardwood floors.

I bend down and touch my finger to a gash in the floor. The bitch took a knife to that, too. Fucking hell.

I enter the kitchen and realize I should have fucking stopped and gone back to the clubhouse. It would have been a better choice. Instead, I stare at every single dish, cup, appliance, utensil, and whatever else is in a kitchen that has been thrown or smashed around the space. A frying pan sits on top of the once glass stove; now it's just shattered pieces. The door to the microwave is off its hinges, too.

This bitch is pissed. Then again, at this moment, so the fuck am I.

I walk quickly through the rest of the house, noting the bitch fucking touched every single room of the house. There is nothing I can even remotely keep. My clothes are tattered pieces of fabric. Anything she could break, she did. There's nothing left.

As the anger bubbles inside of me, I pick up the already destroyed dresser and throw it across the room, only shattering the wood some more. It doesn't help the anger, so I find whatever is at my feet and fling it against the walls. Over and over, I continue to do this until the rage begins to settle, and I catch my breath.

My bikes!

I race out to the garage and throw open the door. Each one of my three bikes is tipped over and smashed. I don't enter the room. I can't. The anger is too much, and I need to get the fuck out of here now.

I don't bother locking the place up; there's nothing for anyone to steal.

I hop on my bike and ride. I try to clear my thoughts, but this time, the ride doesn't help. The fury trembling through me is too much, way too fucking much. I want to kill the bitch. I *will* kill the bitch.

Winding down the road, I head toward the club-house, which is now one of the only things I own that isn't torn or broken.

My heart constricts painfully as a stinging comes through both arms. I can't breathe. I can't get oxygen into my lungs. What the fuck is happening?

My vision blurs as I pull the clutch and release the throttle, shifting down. Suddenly, blackness invades me, which is a good thing when my bike smashes to the pavement.

22

MEARNA

"Mom!" Tanner rushes into the apartment, tears lining her face, which instantly puts me on high mom alert.

"What?"

"It's ... Cam." She sniffles and shakes her head, sucking in a deep breath. I see the moment her spine stiffens, and all the strength that belongs to my Tanner comes into place. "It's Dagger. He's in the hospital. It's bad. We need to go."

Tanner races around the room as I sit there, momentarily in shock. She slips on my shoes and pulls me to my feet just as I snap back to reality.

"What happened?" I ask as she pushes me out the door, holding her purse and mine.

"Car," she orders, putting me in and strapping me like I'm a child, which maybe I am in this moment because I feel a bit lost.

Tanner throws the car into gear, and I hang on to the door for support.

"Talk, Tanner," I tell her curtly.

"Rhys said the doctors think he had a heart attack, but he was riding his bike at the time."

I close my eyes as tears fall from them, and my heart peels layers away from it, broken. No. Shit, no.

"It's bad, Mom. He had a helmet on, which helped, but he was going too fast when he laid out the bike."

"What else?" I ask, my voice low, my stomach already twisting and turning. I'm pretty sure I'm on the verge of throwing up.

Tanner sniffles again, and I snap to her. I didn't even think. Shit. I move my hand to her thigh and begin rubbing it up and down.

"Baby, it will all be okay. Let's just get there and find out what's going on." I try to reassure her. She nods and I lay my head back on the seat.

He can't die. He can't. I just found him again.

Entering the hospital, the stench of dread fills me with each step I take. As we walk down the long, white corridor, the lights are too bright; everything is too bright. Tanner continues to lead me while I follow wordlessly. We enter a large room where Dagger's brothers and their women stand in wait.

Tanner heads straight to Rhys who engulfs her in his arms. Her head rests on his chest as Rhys's eyes close, telling me he needs her just as much as she needs him.

A soft hand comes to my arm, and I turn to see Ma, who gives me her warmth. I take it with her soft words in my ear.

"What's happening?" I pull back, looking at the room. The solemn faces aren't giving me any encouragement.

Pops comes up, pulling Ma in his arms. "He's in

surgery. They have to get a stint in his heart to open a closed artery. Not only that, but he broke his left arm, and they have to go in and repair that." He shakes his head, almost seeming lost in his thoughts. "He's got a hell of a road burn, and they believe he has a concussion. We just have to wait."

Wait. Oh, that's easier said than done.

Tanner wraps her arms around me, hugging me tightly. This is not how this was supposed to go. Not that I had any sort of plan, but him getting hurt was not on that list at all.

———

"FAMILY OF CAMERON WAGNER." A man in a green scrubs with a stethoscope around his neck comes out and looks around the room.

I rise to my feet as the brothers and their women do, too. I tug Tanner close to me, holding her hand for support.

The doctor takes us all in then clears his throat. "Mr. Wagner?"

"Dagger," Rhys says, making the doctor jump, eye him, and then swallow.

"Mr. Dagger. We put the stint in his heart and found no damage, which is excellent. We had to put a metal rod next to his bone." He points to his arm just above his wrist. "It is casted and will remain that way for six weeks. He also has several abrasions to his legs, chest, arms, and face. Those, we treated and are giving him antibiotics."

"So, he's okay?" I ask as Tanner squeezes my hand.

"We need to keep an eye on his brain and make sure

the swelling goes down from the concussion. Other than that, he's a very, very lucky man."

I let out a deep breath then gasp in air. I guess I forgot to breathe there for a bit.

"Can I see him?" I ask.

"Are you his wife?"

I stand there, stunned a moment by the question.

"Yes, she is, and I'm his daughter," Tanner says from beside me, helping me out. I love that girl.

"Give us a couple of hours. He's still very heavily sedated from surgery. We'll come and get you." He gives us a soft smile.

Pops steps forward with his arm outstretched, and the doctor takes it. "Thank you, sir," he says as the other brothers go up one by one and shake the man's hand.

Apprehension creeps in the doctor's eyes, but he holds strong as he turns around and leaves.

I sit back in the chair and hold my head in my hands. I'm too old for this shit. I love him, and I'm going to tell him that as soon as I see him. I'm done wasting time.

23

TANNER

Rhys holds me as we wait for word on Dagger, my father, a man I really know nothing about. That is something that is going to change as soon as he's out of here. Hell, while he's in here. I'll start when I see him. There's no way in hell I want to go the rest of my life having a father and not knowing anything about him: what his favorite food is or color—anything.

My mom is much better now that the doctor has come out. She was trembling there for a bit and starting to scare me. Now she smiles, and the worry lines have softened a bit. Ma sits next to her as they chat. I'm happy for her. She really didn't have many "girlfriends" back home. She needs this.

I look around at all the people who obviously love and care for my father, and my heart swells. I've only ever had my mother, and seeing, watching, talking to everyone makes this a little easier.

"Mr. Wagner?" a woman in scrubs says, her eyes growing wide as she looks at the paper. "I mean, Mr.

Dagger's family." She finally looks up. She doesn't even bat an eye to all of us coming toward her, as if she was warned. Wonder if it told her on the paper.

"Mrs. Dagger?" she asks my mother who nods. "He is still a bit out of it, but you may go back and see him."

"And my daughter?" Mom says, turning to me.

The nurse's gaze hits mine. "It's only supposed to be one, but if one of you leaves pretty quickly, then I'll allow it."

I nod in agreement. I just want to see him physically and know that he's still here on the planet with us.

Rhys kisses my forehead, and then I grab Mom's hand before walking to see my father.

The room is filled with beeping machines making all kinds of different pitched noises. He has tubes coming out of one of his arms, the other in a cast against his chest. Wires come out of every place on his body. His bandana is gone, but his hair is still in its long braid. He has an oxygen mask over his lips and is breathing slowly in and out. The side of his face has bandages on it.

My mother gives me a soft squeeze as the nurse leads us closer.

"Remember, only a few minutes," the nurse tells us, and I nod.

Mom touches Dagger's leg in the one spot that looks like he isn't covered with some type of bandage. Knowing I only have a few minutes, I move to his side.

I lean down and kiss the top of his head gently. "Get better, Dad," I whisper. I then hug Mom and leave the room, tears stinging my eyes. I don't wait; I barge directly into Rhys, and he takes all of my weight as I sob into his shirt.

24

RHYS

After a quick nap, we head back up to the hospital. Dagger is doing well, and the docs say his brain is good. I have to disagree with that, but he's better.

As I enter his room, Dagger's eyes lock on mine. This is the first chance I've had to come in and see him since everything happened. From his set eyes and the anger pouring out of them, I know we need to have a small chat alone.

After Tanner and her father talk for a while, I tell her I need to talk with him. She eyes me suspiciously yet leaves the room. Then I take the chair next to the bed.

"What's going on, brother?"

"I'm alive," he says. "I need you to find Flash. Bitch fucking tore up my house. I mean, there's nothing left! Make sure she understands." He gives me a knowing look and then surprises me. "Give her cash and make sure she stays the fuck away. If she doesn't, then it's the end." He's letting some bitch trash his shit and letting her off?

I nod my head. "You've got it."

"If anything happens to me, you're in charge of my girls. You take care of them." I nod, not letting the shock register. "I mean it. If I don't make it through something, you make sure they are cared for." Damn him.

"Got it."

He turns and looks up at the ceiling for a long time.

I break the silence. "You're out of here tomorrow. I know you have to take it easy, but you're coming to the clubhouse so we can celebrate."

"All right."

TANNER LIES UNDER ME, her eyes full of fresh tears. I just came so hard I saw fucking stars behind my eyes, and she did, too, so why is she crying?

"What's wrong?"

"I love you," she whispers.

The heart that I don't deserve to have, especially after how I made Flash go away earlier today, opens wide for this woman.

Tanner's eyes are shining, and I can feel it deep in my soul. I know I've fucked up more times than I can count, but I'm taking this and fucking running with it.

I place a soft kiss on her lips and brush the tears that have now spilled from her cheeks. "Sprite, love you, too," I whisper softly.

She gasps. "I did—" I place my finger over her lips, silencing her.

"I feel it and wouldn't say shit if I didn't mean it. All the other shit will fall into place."

She nods as I pull my finger away then kiss her breathless.

We lie there, just staring at each other, something I've only done with Tanner, my sprite, and I fucking love this shit.

"Mom wants Dagger to come live at our apartment." It looks like Pops was right. Mearna hasn't left his side for long, so when the discussion of his care came up, Pops thought for sure it would be Mearna wanting that role. "He needs someone to take care of him for a while, and she refuses to let anyone else do it."

I chuckle. Her mom sure is a spitfire. I can see where Tanner gets it.

"That's good."

"Yeah, it is." She snuggles into me, resting her head on my chest.

———

THE GIRLS HAVE BEEN CLEANING up the clubhouse, getting it ready for Dagger's party tonight. He came home earlier today, and Mearna got him settled. She told everyone to stay away so he could rest. She's got a bite to her.

The brothers and I helped move some tables around and brought in a recliner for Dagger to sit in. Ma and Princess have been ordering everyone around while all the ol' ladies help get everything ready.

Arms wrap around my stomach, and just from the feel, I know they belong to my woman.

"Hey, Sprite." I turn her in my arms and plant a kiss on her lips. Fuck wanting other women. No fucking way. Tanner is all the woman I'll ever need. I never thought I could love another human being this much, but each day, it grows. Fuck me, I'm a sap.

"Where's Buzz!" is screamed from the doorway.

"Who's that?" Tanner asks, seeing the black-haired woman who just barged in. Her long hair cascades straight down to her short, white shorts, but it's her look of panic that sets all of us on edge.

"That's Bella. She's Casey's friend from school," I tell her as Princess walks up.

"And she's *friends* with Buzz and Breaker," Princess tells her. "What?" she says, seeing my scowl. "She'll find out sooner or later."

"Both of them?" Tanner gasps, but my focus goes back to the gorgeous woman with jet black hair that I swear has some blue in it. Her eyes are frantic, setting me on guard.

"What's going on, Bella?" Pops comes up and asks.

"Buzz told me that I needed to get here now, so I did. What's going on?"

Pops looks to me then to GT and Cruz. What the fuck?

Buzz bursts through the basement doors, moving right up to Bella and scooping her in his arms, hugging her tightly to his body. His head goes to the crook of her neck.

"Buzz?" Pops asks from behind him.

He pulls away just as Breaker pulls Bella to his front, his arms wrapping around her.

"We need church. Now. I know who it is," he says, and everything comes to a halt.

Fucking shit.

Keep up to date by texting
RYANMICHELE to 444999
for the latest news!

GRAB the next book Captivate Me now! Stay tuned for a sneak peek.

ACKNOWLEDGMENTS

Thank you to my Sinner's group. Your support has meant the world to me. I've enjoyed every moment of getting to know each of you. Thank you. Thank you. Thank you!

To my betas—Lisa, Amber, Lori, and Lisa—thank you for all your hard work on this book. I appreciate every comment, every red mark, every bubble, and every slash.

To Keeana and Elizabeth—thank you for your keen eye.

To Jessica, Kimberly and Ember—thank you for catching what I couldn't see.

To my family, thank you for standing by me while I'm on this journey. Thank you for putting up with the take out, dirty house, and sometimes barely-there mom while I allow my characters to come out of me. I love you, K, P, and D.

Editor: C&D Editing
Cover Designer: Cassy Roop, Pink Ink Designs

ABOUT THE AUTHOR

Ryan Michele found her passion bringing fictional characters to life. She loves being in an **imaginative world** where anything is possible. Her knack for **the unexpected twists and turns** will have you on the **edge of your seat** with each page. She is best known for her **alpha, bad boy bikers** and **strong, independent heroines** in her MC romance books.

When she isn't writing, Ryan is a mom and wife, living in rural Illinois and reading by her pond in the warm sun.

Join my Reader Group: Ryan's Sultry Sinners
Sign up for my Newsletter

COME FIND RYAN:
www.authorryanmichele.com
ryanmicheleauthor@gmail.com

facebook.com/authorryanmichele

twitter.com/Ryan_Michele

instagram.com/author_ryan_michele

bookbub.com/authors/ryan-michele

OTHER BOOKS BY RYAN

www.authorryanmichele.com/books

Ravage MC Series

Ravage MC Rebellion Series

Sealed in Strength
Connected in Code

Power Chain: Anti-Hero Game
Power Chain
PowerHouse
Power Player
PowerLess
Overpowered

Vipers Creed MC
Crossover
Challenged
Conquering

Ruthless Rebels MC
Shamed
Scorned
Scarred
Schooled
Ruthless Rebels Box Set

Raber Wolf Pack Series
Raber Wolf Pack Book 1
Raber Wolf Pack Book 2
Raber Wolf Pack Book 3
Raber Wolf Pack Series Box Set

Standalone Romances
Full Length Novels
Needing to Fall
Safe

Wanting You
Blood & Loyalties: A Mafia Romance

Novellas
Stood Up (Billionaire Up Romance)

Short Stories
Hate to Love
Branded
Bangin'

www.authorryanmichele.com/books

Thank you for reading!

Ryan
Michel